Waking Amelia

SHINA JAMES

WRITER'S TREE
WRITER'S TREE / SAN ANTONIO

Writer's Tree Publishing

P.O. Box 875

Helotes, TX 78023

www.writerstreepublishing.com

First Edition: January 2019

ISBN- 978-0-9961221-4-6 (Paperback)

Dedicated to those who have loved

dangerously

The mob within the heart

Police cannot suppress.

The riot given at the first

Is authorized as peace,

The Mob within the Heart

Emily Dickinson

BOOK 4

"Aaron"

Prologue

The melodic tones of the third bell only enhanced her surroundings, leaving her unable to react to its intention. She could practically taste the sweet fruit from the trees and the freshly made honey at a nearby beehive. Under normal circumstances, she would've run and never looked back—but not here. She rested her head in the soft grass and pondered the last conversation she'd had. He'd walked up and stood directly in front of the sun. There was something familiar to her about his smell and the way his hair blew in the wind. Amelia sat up, took a breath, and then took another. She stood up, and the boy held out his hand. His lips parted, but she held two fingers to her lips, indicating he need not speak. She stared into his deep blue eyes—that was all the introduction she needed. She knew exactly who he was and held out her arms.

Aaron

Chapter One

Howling winds brush against Amelia's window, taunting Aaron. He would give anything to get a whiff of the two a.m. breeze instead of being trapped in a room, inhaling the same suffocating stale air as Leona. Sweat emanates from his pores and clings to his clothes. Leona, livid, shifts her glare from Aaron to Amelia before she finally steps back and leaves the room.

Aaron's eyes remain glued to the door until he is certain Leona is down the hall; then, he goes into the bathroom and splashes cold water on his face. He looks into the mirror—his reflection stares back at him, and he seriously considers punching it in the face. At that moment, he understands his own fury and realizes he was about to kill Leona with his bare hands. That realization changes everything.

He goes back to bed and holds Amelia in his arms until she falls asleep. Then he eases out of bed, takes his phone out of his pocket, quietly strolls out onto her back porch, and makes a call.

"What time is it? Are you alright son?" Mason asks through a yawn.

"It's pretty late, Dad. But I wanted to let you know that I'll be at Amelia's for a while, maybe even a few days. I'm really worried about her, and I have to make sure she's safe."

"Safe? Safe from what? I'm worried about you, Aaron. Just hours ago, you lost your mother—I think you should be with your family."

"I'm fine. If I need anything I'll call, but just give me a couple of days," Aaron whispers.

"I don't know what's going on with Amelia, but I know you guys are hiding something. Is there anything I need to know?"

Aaron bangs his head against his fist and responds, "No. I'll talk to you soon, Dad, I love you."

"Alright…I guess. I love you too, son. Goodnight."

Aaron hangs up abruptly and paces back and forth. He wants to break something—anything. He hates lying almost as much as he hates Leona. He knows his dad can never know what is really going on here. If he did, Aaron would be forbidden to step foot anywhere near Amelia, and that can never happen. He moves from the porch to their favorite tree. Fallen leaves dance through the air as the cool breeze awakens the backyard. Every event that has come to pass since the first time he saw her face races through his mind like a fast-forwarded movie. Her piercing blue eyes have so much life, even though they're hiding the most horrific secrets.

She has suffered so much, he considers. Broken bones, contusions, and bruises—and that's just the physical part. "What have I done," he whispers as tears pool his eyes. *I should've trusted my gut instead of placating her.* Feeling physically ill and ashamed of himself, he pulls his phone back out of his pocket, hoping to be the one to end this for good. He knows he can't let this go on any longer and refuses to see another bruise on Amelia's beautiful body.

Crack!

He whirls around just as a dark figure lunges for him. They tussle in the grass, rolling and punching until Aaron victoriously straddles the masked stranger and grabs a large rock. He grits his teeth and raises his weapon in the air.

Suddenly, a sharp prick stabs his arm. He pauses. His sense of smell disappears. The rock slips from his fingers. *Plunk!* He helplessly falls on his back and stares at the dark, starry sky until it slowly fades to away.

*****

The corners of Leona's mouth lift into a smile. Mason hands her a cup of black coffee. She lightly blows the steam and sips slowly. Mason clasps his hands together and rests his elbows on the mahogany table.

"I can't express how sorry I am for your loss. Gisel was an amazing woman," Leona says and takes another sip.

His lips form a hard line, and he rubs his bloodshot eyes. Leona notices the purple, puffy bags beneath and realizes he hasn't slept much, if at all. The only time she's ever felt remotely close to what he must feel was when her father died. She remembers that day as if it was hours ago. She will never forget how empty she felt inside. She was aware of the puffiness and soreness of her own eyes. She understands how grief can transform the most beautiful person into a washed up entity within minutes; as if pain is something to be worn.

"Thank you. I appreciate you coming by this morning," Mason utters.

"Amelia informed me last night, and I must say, my heart sank when I heard the news. Losing a spouse is never easy. I wish I could say it'll get easier, but it never does. You just learn to live with it." She takes another sip of coffee and peers down at her watch.

"Well, not to be insensitive—I never wanted to be a part of this club. I suppose nobody wants to be, but I always assumed that I would be the one to go first since Gisel was a few years younger than me," Mason says. He wipes away a tear and looks over his shoulder. "You know, I still expect her to come walking out of the room. I can practically hear her fussing at me for putting too much sugar in my coffee…and this is just day one." He brings a tissue to his nose and rubs it red.

Leona pats his hand. "You'll be okay, Mason. Just take it one day at a time. If there ever was a time for you to be vulnerable, this is it." She checks the time again and slowly rises from her chair. "Just let me know if there's anything you need."

"Actually there is. I got a call from Aaron late last night, and I would appreciate it if you would look after him for me. He claims to be fine, but I know he's hurting. He and

Gisel had this unbreakable bond. It angers me that he's trying to be tough when I know he must feel lost. Nonetheless, he wants to be with Amelia, and I know she's good for him. I hope it's okay that he's there."

Leona grimaces and then smiles. "Of course it's okay. Aaron is no trouble at all. I'll take good care of him. Don't worry about anything."

"Thank you," he says. He straightens and walks her out. She hugs him goodbye and rushes to her car. She pulls out her phone and sends a text message.

Mason turns to walk back inside, but not before blowing a kiss into the bright sky. "Rest in Heaven, honey," he whispers.

*****

While still puffing from a bastard of a run, Brady opens the door to his apartment and reluctantly walks in. He leans against the door and wonders just how long he's going to have to keep up this persona. Some days are easier than others, but today feels off, and regardless of the run, he finds it hard to breathe. His line of work has always been demanding; some jobs last a few months while others may last a year. But this particular assignment vexes him. If he could crawl out of his skin, he would: that's what bothers him the most. He takes a bottle of water from his fridge and swigs half of it in one gulp.

Being a cop was insufferable most days. He'd threatened to quit numerous times - more than he could count - every time another criminal went free. But it was all part of the job, and eventually he grew a thick skin. He'd come to accept that the justice system was warped and all he could do was his job as best he could. He'd learned the hard way that some things were just beyond his control, which is what got him through for thirty years. When he decided to retire and become a private investigator, he knew he'd found his true calling. This job satisfied the phantom itch in his life that he needed to scratch. He was so effective that he single-handily turned countless criminals over to the police. He presented them with so much evidence it was virtually impossible that the culprits were ever getting out of jail. He took pride in his success—until now.

After a year on the case, he is losing faith in himself and is frustrated that he doesn't have what he needs to put Leona behind bars—no body, no witnesses, and no real evidence, which means no case. Navid is his only hope, but he has disappeared. *If I can't get a hold of the one person who can put Leona away, then this is a lost cause*, he laments. Still, he is not ready to give up; he wouldn't be able to live with himself if she is allowed to live out the rest of her days as a free woman. The extensive amount of time he has spent with her has only heightened his longing for justice.

His phone rings. He cringes when he sees who's calling, but answers it anyway.

"Brady, please tell me you've got something," the woman says.

He leans against the edge of the kitchen table and takes a deep breath. "Ramona, if I had anything to share I would've called you."

"That witch killed my brother, Brady! It's been an entire year and you've come up with nothing. I'm not paying you to find serenity."

"Serenity? I've been busting my butt to find any piece of evidence, but all I have is a damn earring." He cradles the phone and massages his temples.

"An earring? We can't do squat with an earring. Oh my gosh; this isn't happening," Ramona whispers through tears.

"I know you're hurting Ramona, but don't give up on me. I can do this."

"I'm sorry Brady, but I don't have much faith that you can. What bugs me the most is that I never liked Leona. I told Roland that she's no good; something about her radiated evil.

But then she got pregnant, and I knew that he was going to stay because that's the type of person he was. Now that he's gone, I have to live with the fact that she killed him and there is nothing I can do about it."

"Believe me, I know how hard it must be to go every day without closure for what happened to Roland. But we're close. I feel it…I know it. You're just going to have to trust me on this."

"Trust you? I've trusted you for a year and we have nothing! I can't keep paying you when I know Leona is going to get away with it. I'm pulling the plug…I'm sorry."

"No! That's the last thing you should do when we're so close. Listen, I didn't want to say anything because I didn't want to get your hopes up, but your nephew, Navid, he has agreed to testify."

"What do you mean? He knows what happened to his father?"

"I believe he does. But that's all I can tell you." He sighs, wets a paper towel with cold water, and plants it on his forehead. He places a toe behind the opposite heel and removes his shoes from his throbbing feet.

"Just how long have you been sitting on this piece of news? I mean, all this time you could've had the case reopened, and you did nothing," Ramona implores.

"No, it's not like that. I found out not too long ago. It took some convincing to get him to even agree to do it. I've just been waiting for the right moment to strike and gather as much evidence as I can."

"Right moment? Now is the right moment! You need to call the police," she demands.

"Ramona…it's complicated. For one thing, I can't get a hold of Navid: he's disappeared. I just hope he hasn't changed his mind. The last thing I need is for him to blow me off. But regardless, I can't go to the police until I have everything I need."

"I don't know, I think you're stalling. If I didn't know any better, I would think you're enjoying all of this."

"Enjoying this? Are you serious? Do you know what I've had to do? I have been doing everything I can to keep that psychopath from suspecting anything while I find a way to put her behind bars. I've spent a year of my life doing this for you and your family so that you can find peace—a year I will never get back. Maybe I'm the one who should pull the plug."

"No, Brady, please don't. I'm sorry. I realize that this can't be easy on you either. To be honest, I feel sorry for anyone who has to be anywhere near that woman. I just hope that whatever you have and whatever you're working towards will be sufficient."

"I can't explain what I feel, but I know we're close. We'll get her Ramona."

"Oh, I am praying that's so, Brady. We've waited a long time for this and I want it done right. Forgive me?"

"No need. I'd be just as upset as you are. Listen, I have to go, but I'll be in touch. Bye now."

After hanging up, Brady trades his water bottle for a bottle of tequila he has stowed in the cabinet. He downs a shot and hopes that he was convincing enough. The last thing he needs is for Ramona to get involved or call the police herself. He knows he has to finish this case and fast.

He takes another shot…and then another. He's almost entirely inebriated when he receives a text message from Leona, stating she'll be busy for a couple of days, but wants to go to dinner Friday night. Just for kicks, he makes a call.

The phone rings once and then answers: *"Hi you've reached Navid, leave a message."*

*****

Aaron opens his eyes and turns to his side to breathe. His heart is hammering against his chest and his head is throbbing. He rubs his arm and feels a tiny bump. He can barely see his hands in front of him it's so dark. A musty smell is causing his stomach to churn. He gets to his knees and vomits into an old container nearby. He wipes his mouth, looks around, and tries to remember how he got here in this unfamiliar room. The last thing he remembers is holding Amelia.

"Amelia!" he screams. "Hello? Can anyone hear me?"

He jerks forward when the contents in his stomach sear his throat and spew out of his mouth, barely giving him time to react. He reaches for an old ratty blanket to wipe his mouth when he notices someone's feet sticking out from under it. He rubs his eyes and looks down at the person towards him. "Oh my God! Navid!"

He starts to panic and staggers back to the door, banging on it until his knuckles bleed. "Help me!"

He looks back at Navid's motionless body and bangs again. "Please help us," he cries.

He walks back slowly to Navid and props his head with the old blanket. Navid's body is still warm, but there's no pulse. He leans over him and puts his ear to Navid's nose. No air escaping.

"Okay, okay I can do this. Hold on Navid," he screams in his ear. He starts with thirty chest compressions and gives two rescue breaths before repeating a second time. He checks his neck for a pulse after the third round of chest compressions and feels the carotid artery thumping against his fingers. "A pulse, oh thank God. You're going to be okay," he whispers.

Navid is still unconsciousness, but his chest is slowly moving up and down as shallow breaths escape his lips.

Click!

Someone unlocks the door and tugs hard at the jammed hinges. Aaron quickly covers Navid with the blanket, realizing that it was no accident that he was left for dead. He hides behind a wardrobe trunk and picks up a wooden cane on the floor next to it.

Boston, MA

September 20, 1990

Chapter Two

Dr. Taylor turned onto his side for what seemed like the hundredth time that night. His eyes met the only thing he could see in the pitch-black room. Crimson numbers blinked 5:35 AM on his radio clock. He sighed. *No snoozing today,* he thought. He had a night of interminable reveries about his future and not a single amount of sleep. All he could do was recite his "thank you" speech over and over until it was something he could say in his sleep, if he got any. He promised himself that today was going to be the first day of the rest of his life. He grinned and pulled back the sheets, took a hot shower, and called for room service. He wanted to indulge in every way, right down to the food he was going to eat. After all, he deserved it.

With his stomach bulging, he shoved the last bite of his blueberry pancake into his mouth and groaned as the amalgam of syrup and butter coated his tongue. He washed it all down with a scorching cup of Colombian roast, and then got up and donned his brand new gray suit jacket. He left the room and rode the elevator down to the lobby.

"Good morning, Dr. Taylor. I hope you had a restful night," the receptionist said.

"No my dear, it wasn't restful at all." Seeing her smile fade, he added, "My excitement wouldn't let me sleep."

"Oh, of course. Shall I call you a cab?"

"No, I have a car waiting. Thank you."

He strolled out of the revolving doors and was disappointed that his car wasn't there. He checked his watch and stood there waiting patiently until his patience began to break away like clouds after a rainstorm. He looked down the street—no one was coming. He removed his glasses and was rubbing the bridge of his nose when someone rushed by and almost knocked him down.

"Watch it, jerk!" he shouted.

He cleaned his lenses with a handkerchief and sulked as he watched people around him move like brainless idiots. *Where the hell were they all going?* Surely his engagement was more important than theirs. He'd spent years perfecting his work with countless experiments and sleepless nights, and the results were life-changing. He glanced at his watch for the fourth time and paced until a black stretch limousine pulled up to the curb. He gritted his teeth, envisioning some celebrity stepping out in an Armani suit or a Chanel dress, getting the royal treatment when he created something that could save lives. He deserved the respect that he wasn't getting and it infuriated him as stood there waiting.

The driver got out and hurried to the other side of the limo. Dr. Taylor pursed his lips and crossed his arms as his blood boiled, until he noticed a woman standing about seven feet away from him. The first thing he saw was her mile-long legs elegantly tucked into a pair of shiny black stilettos. The essence of her jasmine perfume soared straight to his nose. He wondered if he was the only soul who could smell it. He appreciated the way her floral wrap-dress emphasized her curves and how her brown hair cascaded just passed her shoulders. Finally, they locked eyes, and her pursed lips became a smile.

He craned his neck to his left and his right.

She smirked and removed her shades.

The blood drained from his face. He couldn't take his eyes off of her, even though he knew he should.

"Moira? What are you doing here?" he whispered, embarrassed.

"I couldn't let you go alone, sir. Not on today of all days," she replied.

"You look amazing. I'm glad you're here. Now everything feels—right." He took her hand and kissed it as thoughts ran wild in his mind. She looked deep into his eyes and then pulled him towards the limo where they drove off to one of the most important meetings of their lives.

On the ride over, Moira could barely contain her excitement and seriously considered jumping into his lap. She'd never been attracted to him before; after all, their relationship was completely professional. But there was something extremely sexy about him getting the one thing he'd worked so hard for, heck they'd worked so hard for. It seemed like it was just yesterday when she started her first day on the job at Linehart Hospital.

*****

Fresh out of medical school, she arrived in New York City in the dead of winter and was certain she would freeze to death before getting a chance to exercise her skills. Moira had graduated at the top of her class and wouldn't dream of letting Mother Nature stop her from doing what she loved—her dream job. As she entered the hospital, she felt a surge of excitement just thinking about all she was going to learn and experience. The moment her feet hit the linoleum floor, she felt at home. Linehart Hospital, owned by TKM Enterprises, was one of the best hospitals in the country. She was going to be a part of a place where world-renowned doctors practiced medicine and saved lives every day. She took a deep breath, smoothed out her scrubs, and donned her impeccably white jacket. She clipped on her badge and admired the blue stitching above the pocket: *Dr. Moira Smith.* It would be a fast-paced year for this first-year resident.

Just as she was heading towards the nurse's station, a patient ran up with his arm sliced open, begging for someone to help him. A nurse ran over with a wound kit. Moira threw on some gloves and quickly sprang into action as the patient stumbled back and splattered blood all over her new white coat. The nurse and an orderly got the man onto a gurney. Moira bit her lip, removed her jacket, and stitched the patient's arm. The rest of the day was just as hectic, and by the end of her first day she was exhausted but happy with the flow and the morale of the hospital. She was charting her last patient when someone tapped her on the shoulder. She glanced over her shoulder and froze.

"I don't believe we met. I am Doctor…"

"I-I know who you are," she stuttered. "Doctor Taylor, it is an honor to meet you. I mean, you are a genius," she said while awkwardly shaking his hand. "We talked about you in school. I can't believe you're here. Your work on Neurodegeneration is mind-blowing. Oh, and congratulations on your latest award." She realized she was fawning and blushed.

He chuckled. "Thank you. It's nice to have a fan. You know science is all about experiments, finding what works, and most of all, dedication. With the right tools, you can do just about anything."

"I agree, but don't be so modest. Not everyone can do what you've done at such a young age. Sir, you're incredible," Moira declared.

He shoved his hands in his pockets and grinned. "Are those your notes?" he asked, reaching for her tablet. He scanned them quickly.

She took slow, deep breaths and clasped her hands together.

"Moira, I must say, I have a good feeling about you. Why don't you shadow me tomorrow?"

She all too eagerly shook her head yes.

"I'll make sure you're in every operating room alongside me, and if you're as astute as I think you are, I'll give you a sneak peek at my latest invention in the lab."

"For real? I mean, I would be honored, sir."

"Great, I'll see you tomorrow morning," he whispered and marched off.

Her head was spinning, and she really had to pee. She glanced at the wide-eyed nurses and shrugged her shoulders.

"Do you know who that was?" one nurse blurted out.

"Of course I know. My armpits are sweating for goodness sakes," Moira replied.

"I'll bet. He never talks to anyone like that. And did you notice is smoldering brown eyes?"

"Honestly, I'm more enamored with his brain than his eyes…but his eyes weren't bad," she giggled.

The nurse shook her head and let out a low chuckle.

*****

The next morning, Moira met up with Dr. Taylor in the operating room. It felt as if some force was pulling them together, and they became the perfect team. She became so immersed learning from him that before long, she could finish his sentences. His brilliant mind always surpassed her expectations and she never tired of hearing him speak. She found herself unable to focus on anything, except him. He trusted her with his work and his notes, and most of all he respected her. She often wondered why he chose her, but could never get the courage to ask for fear of him coming to his senses and realizing she was an insignificant compared to him. Sometimes she found herself thinking about him in ways she shouldn't, and she immediately suppressed her feelings.

For four years, they focused on their work, and nothing more.

*****

"So what do you think?" Dr. Taylor asked.

"Sir?" she replied, flushed.

"Where were you a minute ago?" he asked.

She could only stare into his eyes and realize that no matter how strong her feelings grew for him, she was in over her head. There was no way he felt the same way.

"I was wondering if you'd like to have dinner with me after the meeting?" he offered.

Her heart skipped a beat, and she instinctively leaned over and kissed him on the cheek.

"I'll take that as a yes," he said through a laugh.

They pulled up to a charcoal gray skyscraper with a TKM Enterprises ornament at the top. A sudden wave of silence moved about the limo. Dr. Taylor removed a silk handkerchief from his inner jacket pocket and dabbed his forehead a few times. His mind poured with words, but not a single one escaped his lips. He felt as though his brain lost all communication with the rest of his body. The hairs on his legs rose just as he felt a rivulet glide from his armpit. The toll of a sleepless night left him lethargic, and he was painfully unsure how to buck up. But he knew it would be okay with the help of his right-hand woman.

They entered the building hand in hand. He paused.

"What's wrong?" Moira asked.

"I just want to remember everything about this moment. I want to remember the hint of cinnamon in the air from fresh baked cookies, and I want to remember the smell of bleach and fresh paint. I don't want to be so obsessed with today that I don't remember small things like this."

"In that case, let's cement this occasion." She pulled out her cell phone and snapped as many pictures as she could. He perked up and posed for her. He even smiled on a few. She couldn't be more proud of him and his accomplishments.

"This is such a good idea. Now I want some with you. Get over here," he murmured.

She took several selfies with him and even captured one where he planted a kiss on her cheek. She faced him and stepped closer, but before she could reach up and kiss him, they were interrupted.

"Dr. Taylor, welcome. I'm John, the building manager." Dr. Taylor hesitantly pivoted and reached out his hand to shake John's.

"Hello, it's nice to meet you. This is Dr. Moira Smith, my colleague."

"Hello madam. Before I escort you to the conference room, may I offer you two a glass of lemon water?"

"No thank you," they both replied.

"Excellent, right this way," John said.

Dr. Taylor and Moira giggled quietly as they followed John down a long corridor. They entered the elevator and rode up to the fifteenth floor. There were several plush chairs along the walls of the ornate hallway, and Moira took her seat in the one nearest the conference room. As Dr. Taylor stepped into the room, he turned and took one more look at her.

She mouthed, *good luck.*

As the door closed, he looked around the room and took his seat. His heart was pounding, and his armpits were producing a waterfall underneath his jacket. Eight people sat around the table. One in particular was unexpected. He was stunned and confused. His attempt to remain calm vanished in a single breath as he stared at the woman who had made his life a living hell for three years.

"What the hell are you doing here Judith?"

Aaron

Chapter Three

Aaron never thought that an old brittle cane would be his lifeline in battling a possible murderer. Although his sweaty palms are caked with dirt, he maintains a firm grip. He remains still as a corpse, even calculating the right moments to breathe in and out. His heart hammers against his chest and the room was is dim as a cave, but he is not going to give up without a fight.

Whoever the person is on the other side of the murky wall is getting closer, tiptoeing on the cement floor. Aaron crouches down, waiting for the right moment, but he realizes there isn't one. He steps forward and takes the biggest swing of his life. He doesn't miss.

Two sounds allow him a brief respite. The first from hitting his adversary in the head—the cane splits from the attack and the sound ricochets off the walls. The second sound is the loud thud of the man hitting the floor. Dust sweeps up and feathers Aaron's nose, making it hard to hold in a sneeze. He covers his nose with his shirt and bolts for the door—it's jammed.

He turns the knob and pushes hard, using all of his weight, but it wouldn't budge. He rests his hands on his knees. It's getting harder to breathe in such a confined space. If he doesn't get out soon, he knows he could die. He takes a step back and runs into the door—it moves an inch but does not fully open. *One more forceful thrust should do it,* he thinks. He takes four steps back and runs forward. He trips over a book and hits his head on the door. Surprisingly, the door swings open.

He ignores the throbbing pain and stumbles out, and then realizes that Navid is still lying unconscious. The person responsible is there. Seeing stars, he turns and goes back. Alarm bells are going off in his head like sirens on a fire truck, causing him to walk with purpose. He wants to get Navid and escape but knows he can't leave without knowing who is responsible for this calamity; not knowing the truth will eat at him forever.

He kneels down to check Navid's pulse and feels the steady thump of his carotid artery. Navid's hand twitches under the blanket, but he never opens his eyes. "Navid, wake up," Aaron whispers.

Navid's eyes race back and forth beneath his eyelids.

Aaron knows it won't be long before Navid regains consciousness.

Aaron stands and strolls carefully and quietly to the man face down on the floor. With the door ajar, there is just enough light for him to see more clearly. He picks up a piece of the broken cane. The edge is sharp and could very easily serve as a knife if need be. He nudges the man with his foot and slowly turns the body over. The bloody gash on the stranger's forehead has painted a crimson hue over ninety percent of his face. Even with the blood, Aaron realizes that this man is no stranger. Aaron can't believe his eyes.

He is instantly afraid—of himself. His fingers shake as he grips the cane tighter. His eyes well with tears. He has never killed anyone before. But in this instance, it would be self-defense, and he's positive that there isn't a soul alive who would miss Eli Jamison, the coward.

He glances at an unconscious Navid and paces. His actions will have consequences. Navid may very well hate him if he takes Eli's life. He is conflicted and hates that Navid will only be a few feet away when it goes down.

Maybe it's a good thing he's unconscious, he thinks as he straddles Eli. He raises the sharp edge of the cane in the air. He wants Eli's death to be quick and epic. He inhales a slow and tasteful breath and closes his eyes; every evil thing Eli has ever said or done races through his mind. The last straw was the way he grabbed Amelia's arm and then threw her down like she was trash. Aaron hates Eli and is now uncharacteristically elated that the world will be rid of one less psycho. His arms flash down faster than he thought possible. Then he stops. He swallows hard and breaks out in a cold sweat; the sharp edge of the cane is half an inch from Eli's neck. He sits back and sighs.

Aaron has always prided himself of not being a wimp, never backing away from a fight. But before he does something so drastic, so final, he needs to see Eli's eyes. He needs him to be afraid and know what is coming. He stands up and turns to leave when Eli grabs his leg and forces him down.

Aaron lands on his arm but manages to punch Eli in his wound.

"Ahh!!" Eli cries out and flings Aaron away from him. He rises to his feet and picks up the broken cane.

"I'm going to kill you!" Aaron hollers. He jumps up and runs toward Eli. He tackles him. Eli falls, and Aaron throws his fist into Eli's nose. Blood pours out as Eli wraps his fingers around Aaron's neck.

Aaron struggles to breathe and digs his nails into Eli's gash and making him pause, but it's not enough to stop him. Aaron is strong and wills himself to keep his eyes open as he reaches for anything he can use as a weapon. The room is spinning as the intense pressure on his neck gets worse. He feels as if his life is slowly being squeezed out of him and, he begins to feel defeated.

He stares into Eli's eyes. There is no soul; Eli is as evil and demented as Leona. Aaron continues to pound on Eli's arms and fight for air. His heart beats loudly in his ears, and he's exhausted. He thinks it's all over when he reaches out again and connects with something small and sharp. He grabs it and stabs Eli in the neck.

"Damn you!" Eli screams. He pulls out a springhead nail. Blood seeps between his fingers.

Aaron gasps for air and crawls to a corner, rubbing his neck and gagging. He catches his breath, charges at Eli and pounces on him, slamming Eli's head against the floor repeatedly until he passes out.

Aaron wipes his face and takes a deep breath. Now that he knows who is behind all this, he becomes resolute. He is now on a mission: more intent than ever to expose Leona and Eli, but he needs to hurry. He rummages through old boxes and matted blankets in search for his cell phone. He even checks Navid's pockets.

Aaron's face is wet with sweat when a sudden cold chill comes over him. He finds it difficult to even swallow and runs to the door for air. He opens it and meets Leona's golden eyes.

The blood drains from his face, and his lungs close. He can't breathe. He begins to move back wordlessly, but his mind is telling him that he's going the wrong way. He can't process what's happening. Everything is silent. His back hits the wall, startling him. He has nowhere else to go, although his feet are still moving. If he didn't know better, he'd swear that he was being controlled remotely. He presses his hands by his sides, glares at Leona, and struggles not to pass out.

His head is spinning and his whole body throbs. He closes his eyes and thinks of Amelia and how beautiful she is. As the seconds pass, he knows his future is slowly disappearing. He is determined to think of Amelia one last time. Her bright blue eyes staring back at him calms him as he leans against the wall. Suddenly, Amelia's eyes fade as he opens his own eyes and sees Leona stepping closer with a gun pointed at his chest.

Dr. Taylor

Chapter Four

A deafening silence came over the conference room. Dr. Taylor's throat constricted as he struggled to swallow his own saliva. His peers were strategically planted around the ten-foot table that now seemed to be inches long. Every eye in the room was on him, but his eyes were cemented on Judith. He couldn't look away. The walls began to close in around them until they were all submerged into a melting pot of hate. Judith slammed her pen down and stood up.

She leaned forward and pursed her lips before she spoke. "I am the newest member of the board, Addison, and I have a right to be here. Won't you have a seat so that we can get on with the meeting?"

"You will address me as Doctor Taylor," he stated. He lowered into his chair and sat back, crossing his arms in front of his chest. He glanced at each board member until the color in their faces returned to normal.

Dr. Mark Peters said, "Before we get started, I'd be remiss if I didn't extend my gratitude to you, Dr. Taylor. We've been friends for quite a long time, and within that time I have seen you do the impossible. You're a brilliant neurosurgeon with an extraordinary gift, and I've learned a lot from you. There aren't enough words to express how much we value and appreciate your expertise. Your work has changed lives forever, and we know you will continue to do great things."

"Thank you, Mark. That means a lot," Dr. Taylor replied.

He shifted in his chair and waited for someone to cut the undeniable tension in the room. He was convinced that Judith must have somehow schemed her way into this position. He shouldn't be surprised; he somehow knew that this day would come. He tucked his hands in his soggy armpits, although he really wanted to wrap them around her neck. It was difficult sitting across from her and act like the last three years weren't hell for him. He didn't want her, and instead of accepting it she chose to undermine him and make him miserable.

"Let's call this meeting to order. We'll try to be as brief as we can Dr. Taylor, I understand that you've been waiting a long time for this," Dr. Gloria Senegal declared.

Dr. Taylor nodded and laid out his business plans and expectations for the future. He worked day and night assiduously to create the perfect slideshow and even hired an architect to construct a mock blueprint of his vision.

"Your presentation is exquisite and very detailed. I can practically smell the fresh paint," Dr. Peters said.

"Thank you. I wanted each of you to understand how important this is for me. I take my work very seriously; my patients are my inspiration. If I could build my own hospital wing and state-of-the-art lab, it would not only be beneficial to the hospital, but it would grant me the tools I need to perpetuate my success and create more life-changing cures."

"I think we can all agree that you are an exceptional physician. But I don't think the hospital is ready for this multi-million dollar commitment. We just renovated the psychiatric wing, and I feel that it would be irresponsible to take this on right now," Judith stated.

"Irresponsible? I can assure you that what I am proposing will be the best thing for Linehart Hospital and we all know that when I'm passionate about something I get it done."

"What's wrong with the lab we already have? It's served you well thus far. You and your assistant seem to get along just fine working on experiments day and night," Judith quipped.

"Her name is Dr. Moira Smith, and she's an excellent surgeon. This hospital is lucky to have her, and she's helped me a great deal. Because of her, I can spend more time with my patients." He rolled his eyes. "I would love to hear from someone else," he added.

A few of the other members expressed their concerns, but Dr. Taylor had the perfect response every time. There was nothing he hadn't prepared for, and he found himself bored by their mundane queries. With eight members on the board, it was finally time to bring it to a vote. His dream was seconds away from becoming a reality.

*****

Moira repeatedly tapped her foot as she scanned her third magazine. The knot in her stomach wouldn't allow her to relax, and the hallway was gradually beginning to spin. She stood up and instantly regretted it. She was suddenly catapulted to her childhood when she rode a roller coaster for the first time; she could practically smell the vomit on her clothes and the screams from the angry families that were covered with her morning breakfast. She fanned herself and took John up on his offer for a glass of lemon water. She gulped the entire glass and paced back and forth. Then the door to the conference room swung open.

"I'm so sorry Addison, maybe we can try again in a few years," Dr. Peters said.

"No! It's that evil woman's fault. She did this to get back at me, and I'm going to file a complaint."

Judith charged out of the room. "You go right ahead, but it still won't change anything. Our decision is for the good of the hospital. It has nothing to do with you," she lectured.

"The hell it doesn't. Do you think I don't know what you did? You maneuvered your way into getting a seat on the board just so that you could deny me what is rightfully mine. You knew I wanted my own lab and you couldn't stand to let me have it."

"Believe it or not Addison, not everything is about you," she seethed.

He stepped closer to her and gritted his teeth. "You and I both know that if you don't get your way, there is nothing anybody can do to stop you."

He stormed off mumbling something under his breath. Moira glared at Judith and ran after him. He barely spoke on the ride back to his hotel. Once they arrived, he sat stoically for a minute and then turned to leave the limo when she grabbed his hand and pulled him down for a kiss. He cupped her chin and kissed her once more before disappearing from the car and into the chaotic mass of people entering the double doors.

A debilitating chill came over her and settled so deep that if she were set on fire, it would still be there. Her reality was starting to fade until all that was left was a blank canvas. Whatever feelings they shared were gone, and their future had somehow been ripped away in the conference room. All she wanted to do was hold him and tell him everything was going to be okay. But she understood that there was nothing he wanted more than that lab and the space to do what he did best. It broke her to see everything crumble around her, and there was nothing she could do to stop it. She wiped away a tear and took a flight back to New York that same night.

*****

Dr. Taylor rushed into his hotel room and shoved his belongings into his suitcase; he didn't stop until every toiletry and sock was packed away. Desperate to leave, he made arrangements to get the next flight out. While he waited for a taxi, he brooded over all of the hard work he put into the hospital and patient care and how it was unappreciated by his own peers. He had been so sure he would get the lab and the space to perform the best experiments in the world. What he had not anticipated was that a jealous witch would shoot it all down. New ideas were already swimming around in his head, desperate for a way out, but he refused to give that hospital anymore of his time. He was not going to make them any richer. He sat there in a numb daze, thinking horrible thoughts and seriously considered tracking Judith down. *Judith isn't worthy of my attention*, he resolved—*nobody is*. No one is worthy of my attention became his new motto.

*****

Dr. Taylor took a leave absence and buried himself in a pile of notes and research, ignoring anything not generated by his own mind. He had towering stacks of journals with ideas awaiting experimentation. Days turned into months, and he found it harder and harder to face anyone: especially Moira. Moira did creep into his thoughts, and he sometimes obsessed over what she must think of him. They never really had their chance, and he couldn't help but wonder what magic could have happened between them. They had become best friends at the hospital, which he figured was half the battle. He shook his head at his own stupidity and put pen to paper. Then he let more time elapse.

Adverse to any outside contact, he had stopped answering his phone or checking his voicemail months ago. One morning, he gathered up the courage to check his voicemails. He was shocked to discover there were over twenty-five messages. Dr. Peters called a few times as well as other colleagues and friends who were concerned about him and his whereabouts. He listened to every call and at the end was despondent that he hadn't heard the one voice he longed for—Moira's. He opened a bottle of scotch and poured himself a glass. *She must really hate me*, he concluded.

For years he hadn't thought about women and their feelings because he was literally married to medicine. Women came along and distracted him for a few hours, but that was all he cared to endure. He delighted in their company in small intervals, but Moira was different. She had been his right hand for so long and supported him in every endeavor. *This unacceptable behavior is all the thanks she gets for her devotion?* he chastised himself.

He showered and hopped into his car, but never put the keys into the ignition.

Aaron

Chapter Five

The rise and fall of his stomach's contents, accompanied by his head spinning, reminded Aaron of an unpleasant time on a merry-go-round. *What is going to happen when this is all over?* he thinks as he stands and scowls blurry-eyed at Leona through the chaos around him.

Her eyes sear into him, and his life flashes before his eyes. He wants to do so many things but is hopeless at his inability to do anything. *Amelia warned me not to threaten Leona*, he remembers, and he wishes that he'd listened. Threatening someone as calculated and cold as Leona requires tremendous thought and execution. *I should've called the police the moment I saw what Leona was doing to my Amelia*, he lamented.

Three earth-shattering words repeat in his head over and over. He detests it because he still wants to believe he has more time. But the words, *It's too late,* weaken his soul. Lethargy consumes his body propped against the wall. His eyelids are heavy and weighted. His lips pulse as they begin to swell. He never thought he would have a gun pointed at his chest. One pull of the trigger means the end of him.

Then he thinks: *After everything Amelia and I have suffered, there is no way I'm going out like this.* He sucks in a deep breath and pushes Leona down.

The gun fires.

Eli jolts up and looks around in a daze.

Aaron manages to grab the gun from Leona and pulls the trigger.

"No!" Eli screams. He hobbles over to Aaron and punches him in the face over and over until he isn't sure if it is Aaron's blood or his own that has splattered all over him.

Aaron's eyes swell shut as he fights for his life. He writhes in pain but manages to hit Eli over the head with an old book. Eli falls on his back, mumbling obscenities. Aaron turns to his side, holding his stomach.

"Get him up," Leona demands.

Aaron floats in and out of consciousness when he hears Leona's voice. She orders Eli to tie him up. He can't see but hears everything. The metallic taste of fresh blood oozes from his busted lips. Suddenly, his mouth is duct-taped shut and his hands are tied behind his back. He is too exhausted to retaliate.

"Let me go," he mumbles under the tape.

Eli continues to follow Leona's orders and tapes Aaron's feet together. Aaron feels moisture dripping down his face. He tries to breathe but has concluded that his nose is broken as blood continues to pour out. He drops his head and prays silently that he will make it out of this. Amelia is in danger, and he's afraid of what they'll do to her with him out of the way.

"That was scary. He could've killed you had there been more than one bullet in that gun. Just for kicks, why wasn't there?" Eli asks.

"Honestly, I wanted to play a little game of Russian roulette. Can you imagine the mental anguish of hearing a gun click over and over, knowing the end is near? I wanted my face to be the last thing he ever saw."

"Geez, Mom, that's ruthless," quips Eli.

"Aaron, I know you can hear me you self-righteous prick," Leona says.

Although feeble, Aaron slowly lifts his head and makes one last attempt to break free. He thrashes and throws his body forward and lands on his face, still attached to a chair. Leona kneels down and whispers something so devastating that he screams out and feels a sharp prick in his arm. His entire body shakes and then goes numb. Eli unties him from the chair and lies him down next to Navid. He paused when he notices how warm Navid's arm is.

"Hey,   Mom?"

"Yes? What is it?" Leona replies.

"Navid is warm. Shouldn't he be cold by now?" Eli asks. He kneels down and shakes Navid to see if he'll react.

"What are you talking about? Navid is dead. He has to be." She walks over to him and puts her hand on his neck.

"Leona! Hello!"

"Oh no, That's Brady. We have to get out of here. Quick, let's go," she insists in a harsh whisper.

Eli covers Navid and Aaron with an old blanket and runs out.

Leona composes herself, smoothes out her hair and clothes and steps out into the dark hallway. She appears behind Brady as he moves down the hallway, searching for them. She wraps her arms around his waist. Brady grimaces and then turns to her.

"Hey, love. How are you?" she asked.

"I'm good. I know you said not to come over for a few days, but I just had to see you."

"It's a nice surprise. Why don't we go out to eat? How's that sound?" she offers.

"Sure. I could eat. Why don't we invite the boys? Where's Navid and Eli?"

"They can't make it: busy. I'll go get dressed, just give me a minute to get ready."

Once Leona is out of sight, Brady creeps upstairs and lightly taps on Navid's door. He does not hear a single sound through the cracks around the door. He stands there and calls Navid's cell. His eyes buck when he hears Navid's phone ring…from Eli's room. He knocks on Eli's door and pushes it open. Eli is singing loudly in the shower. Brady calls the phone again and follows the ring. It's inside a box underneath Eli's bed.

"Brady?" Leona shouts.

He puts the phone back and rushes out of Eli's room. He makes it downstairs just as Leona is coming out of the kitchen.

"Where were you?"

"Oh, I just wanted to ask Eli who won the football game, but he was in the shower." He takes her hand and kisses it. "Are you ready?"

She hesitates. "I just want to make one thing clear. I will not tolerate lying in my relationship. If we're going to be together, I need to be able to trust you completely."

"Where is this coming from? You know you can trust me," Brady replies.

"I know...I do. It's just that, well, I never felt free to be myself around anybody before." She takes his other hand in hers. "What I mean is, I love you, Brady."

Cold, hard reality has slapped him in the face, and his heart drops to his stomach. He tastes bile in his mouth as he hears Ramona's threats in his head. She was certain he was enjoying some crazy tryst with Leona. Even though he wasn't, he now realizes that things have gone too far. As if those three magical words weren't scary enough for a guy to hear, they are even scarier coming from someone as sick and mentally disturbed as Leona.

His entire mission for the past year has been to bring her down. And when he does—there will be no love lost. Yet, he still feels like the biggest jerk in the world.

He thinks of reciprocating Leona's sentiment, but can't form the words. Being a private investigator means that discretion and lying are part of the job. But even *he* can't lie that convincingly. He looks into her big, golden eyes and kisses her passionately, hoping it will be enough to pacify her.

She looks up at him and unbuttons the top four buttons of his shirt, then leads him by the hand toward her bedroom.

He pauses at the door. "Hey, I thought you were hungry," he says, re-buttoning his shirt.

"I am," she replies and kisses him again.

"Shall we go?"

She sighs. "Alright, let's go."

She bites her bottom lip and wonders why he is so set on eating out. He's never denied her advances before. Maybe there's more to him than she thinks. A flashback enters her mind from when Navid told her that Brady couldn't be trusted.

Is he really the man I think he is? she wonders. She reluctantly grabs her purse and opens the door, surprised by who is on the other side.

"Where is my son?" Mason asks.

New York City, NY

February 12, 1991

Chapter Six

Dr. Taylor stared at the dashboard in a daze. Something came over him, and he knew that whatever was going on in his head shouldn't be overlooked. He gripped the steering wheel and sat back, breathing in the fresh new leather of his BMW. He was reeling with excitement, although disappointed that he hadn't made the connection before. He put his keys back in his pocket. He desperately needed to write down the information as it progressively formed like building blocks in his mind. He ran into the house and started writing notes about the brain, its nerves, and how nothing in the body will work properly unless everything is working together. *Just like a car won't work without the engine,* he rationalized. He liked the equivalence. He took out a yellow writing pad and drew out the analogy.

There are so many components of an engine, and each part works together to create a magnificent thing. A can of oil is just that, but without it a car will surely overheat, causing everything to eventually break down.

What if I could find a way to keep the brain going no matter what's happening to the body? he mused.

He began writing about cells and what happens to the nerves when they become damaged. His work on neurodegeneration has served him well thus far. All he needs now was to move forward with more details and research. Then he thought about creating a neurotransmitter for the brain that was indestructible and could serve as the primary source of communication for the entire human body. *Patients who died of brain trauma could've possibly lived if the nerves in their brain were stronger and durable and could still send messages to the rest of the organs*, he theorized. Under his theory, the brain would be nothing more than a protective covering for a tiny, yet powerful transmitter.

*****

In two months' time, Dr. Taylor's living room was transformed into a lab. He had state of the art equipment and even some lab rats that he retrieved from a colleague. His determination to create a neurotransmitter that would never stop working was profound. After doing a few test runs, he came up with nothing. The more he experimented, the more he drank from disappointment. He took the time to eat, shower, and sleep, and thought of nothing except the human body and how everything would come together perfectly with his foreseeable creation.

It took him another three months of working day and night to finally see a finished product. He was confident that what he built would be extraordinary in modern science, especially with this tiny device safely secured inside the brain. Now all he needed to do was to try it out on an actual human body. He thought long and hard about who in their right mind would believe in his vision the way he did. The board of directors wouldn't even give him a lab, so he knew that their support would be out of the question. His only hope was his long-time friend, Dr. Peters. That night after a bout of heavy drinking, he gave his friend a call.

"I'm telling you Mark, what I have created is mind-blowing. Nothing I have ever done in the past compares to this. It will change medicine and everything we know about the human body forever."

"Addison, you don't have to sell me on a thing. As excited as you sound I can't even imagine how remarkable it is. But, what do you need from me?" he asked.

"What I'm about to say is going to sound unethical, and probably illegal. Now, we both know how the laws work when it comes to a new product. It has to be approved by the FDA, we need years and years of research and studies, etc. But I can't wait that long; I'm anxious to see if this will work. What I'm saying is that I need to know that I can trust you and that you can deliver me a specimen."

Dr. Peters cleared his throat. "I don't know Addison. This seems like it's too risky. I mean, you're one of my best friends, but I'm not willing to go to jail for you. You understand that, right?"

Dr. Taylor rolled his eyes. "Yes, I understand, and I wouldn't have asked if I weren't so desperate. And you know I would never in a million years want to put you in jeopardy of losing your license and going to prison. I guess I was just hoping you might have a John Doe who is brain dead and that you would accidentally leave the body unattended while I perform the procedure."

"Why don't you come back to work? Your job will always be there for you. I realize you're still upset about not getting your lab, but at least you would have access to the donors who've given their bodies to science for research," Mark explained.

"No. I can't go back there. They humiliated me in that conference room, Mark. Judith and her minions treated me like I was some second-rate physician with no experience whatsoever. I'm honestly afraid of what I'll do if I see her. Besides, I need a live body, a beating heart," he said. "Look, just forget I said anything. You know what it's like when you have a new toy and you can't wait to try it out. I'll figure it out."

"I'm so sorry man. Your brilliance will never be lost on me, and I'm positive that what you created will be a game changer. I can only hope that when the time comes for you to get yet another award, I'll be there to cheer you on," Mark said.

"Ha! I wouldn't have it any other way. Take care, my friend," Dr. Taylor said and hung up.

*****

Moira heard her name blaring throughout Riverleaf Hospital. She rushed to the OR and scrubbed into her third surgery of the day. She was exhausted, but working was all she had left. Whenever she thought about calling Dr. Taylor, her stomach turned into knots. That cold, chilling feeling from when he got out of the car still lingered, and the heartbreak was still difficult for her to bear. Just thinking about him made it hard for her to breathe. This time, her work as a surgeon would not relieve her angst.

"Time of death: twelve thirty-eight," Moira stated. She slammed her fists on the operating table. An OR nurse removed the breathing tube from the patient's mouth and turned the heart monitor off. Everything fell silent. Moira inhaled deeply, hoping to stop her heart from hammering. Her scrubs stuck to her skin and her throat constricted. Not a single person on her medical team uttered a syllable. She removed her surgical mask and eyewear and walked out in tears. Her third surgery of the day had ended in death. She loathed days like this when nothing good happened. Her job was to save lives, but she couldn't do it today.

"Hey Dr. Smith, how is everything going? Are you getting along with the scheduling? I realize that Riverleaf is small and a far cry from Linehart Hospital, but we hope you will find that we are a thriving facility with brilliant doctors," Dr. Simon Graff said when he saw her in the doctor's lounge.

"Absolutely, Dr. Graff. As strange as this may sound, I feel like this is where I belong. I think I can do great things here. I mean, I'm having a horrible day, but it has nothing to do with the hospital. I'm happy to practice medicine here as long as you'll have me."

"That's what I like to here. Listen, if you need anything just give me a holler. We take excellent care of our surgeons, and I want you to be comfortable to speak your mind and have the freedom to express any concerns."

Moira nodded with a smile. She went to her office to finish her notes. Afterward, she rushed home and opened a bottle of Chardonnay: her daily routine for the past five months. She was finishing her second glass when the news came on. "Breaking News" ran across her television screen.

"Good evening, I am Paloma Ramirez reporting live from Doctor Addison Taylor's residence. Apparently, 911 was called when a friend of Dr. Taylor's found him unresponsive in his home. We don't have any further information at this time, but what we do know is that one of the most brilliant surgeons of our time has died. There will be more details to come."

Endless tears rolled down Moira's face. She wanted to scream, but nothing came out. Her legs began to give way as she struggled to keep herself upright.

For the next three days, she laid in her bed in an almost vegetative state until she heard her front door open. She lifted her head off her pillow and hoped it wasn't a burglar, because she had no energy to fight anyone off. She pulled the covers to her chin and waited for the person's footsteps to stop outside her bedroom door.

"Mom? What are you doing here?" Moira croaked as her mother strolled in.

Her mother sat on the side of the bed and wrapped her arms around Moira. Moira broke down and wailed so hard and loud her face and stomach muscles hurt.

"Honey, I'm so sorry about your friend. I could tell how much you loved him," her mother whispered.

Moira sniffed and wiped her face. "I just don't understand. He was healthy, and he was taking good care of himself. Do you think he was murdered?" Moira asked.

"I hope not. From what I heard on the news it looks like there was no foul play. We'll find out soon enough. I just want to make sure you're okay."

After a couple of days and against her mother's wishes, Moira went back to work and decided to put Dr. Taylor in the back of her mind. She realized that it would be no use spending any more time grieving over someone who didn't think enough of her to call or text. After all, she stood by him through everything, and he'd left her heartbroken.

A week later it was reported that Dr. Taylor died of alcohol poisoning. Moira couldn't believe it. She was devastated that this would be the first thing people were going to remember when they heard his name. She shed a few more tears and vowed to get her life back on track.

*****

A month went by, and she finally found her niche at Riverleaf Hospital. She went on to perform many successful surgeries and procedures. She even stepped foot in one of their labs and took notes about patient care and planned to follow in her mentor's footsteps. After all, she could never deny how much Dr. Taylor had taught her. She intended to go very far with what she now knew and even dreamed about getting an award or two of her own one day.

Just as she finished charting her last patient one evening, her cell phone rang. She didn't recognize the number but answered anyway. "Hi, is this Dr. Moira Smith?"

Silence.

She wasn't sure what to say. She bit her bottom lip and thought very hard about hanging up. She figured it was probably one of those telemarketers, or perhaps it was some receptionist begging her to attend some medical conference. She always went to those with him—and that was no longer an option. Tears pooled her eyes. *Dammit!* She angrily wiped them away.

"Who is this?" she said again into the phone.

"I'm sorry if I disturbed you, ma'am. I realize you're a busy woman, so I'll be brief. My name is Shane Walsh. I am Dr. Taylor's lawyer. I would like to meet with you at your earliest convenience to discuss Dr. Taylor's estate."

Aaron

Chapter Seven

It wasn't very often that Leona had nothing to say. She always had a plan B and could think of a lie within the blink of an eye, but looking into Mason's heartbroken eyes—not this time.

She can feel the little pockets of sweat on her hands and forehead. After everything she's gotten away with to this point, she is absolutely stunned that she is even considering confessing and going to jail—because, shockingly, she can't lie to Mason. Suddenly, she understands that he is her weakness. She isn't afraid of him, but there is something about him that undermines her with guilt, and there is nothing she can do about it. Her eyes water and her hands are so wet that Brady lets go and stares at her.

"Leona," Brady whispers, "are you alright?"

Her lips tremble as she sobs, "I'm so sorry. You see…Aaron is…"

"Hey Mason, how are you doing?" Eli calls out as he hurries downstairs.

Mason's eyes slide from Leona's. He strolls passed her and Brady and crosses his arms.

Eli motions for them to go into the living room. They sit across from each other.

"I'm so sorry for your loss, sir. Mrs. Gisel was a very kind woman and will be greatly missed," Eli whispers.

"Thank you, Eli. Listen, I don't want to take up too much of your time." He checks his watch and stands up. "But I was looking for Aaron, where is he? Micah has been asking about him a lot, and he's not answering his cell phone. I need to know he's okay."

"Oh, uh, he and Amelia went out to eat. It was my idea to treat them to a dinner and movie. Amelia wanted to find a way to distract him, so we're hoping it will work. We're taking good care of him; I'll make sure he gives you a call when they get back," Eli assures him.

"Oh, okay I appreciate that. I suppose this will be a good thing for him. I better go before he comes back and sees me; I certainly don't want to make him feel worse. Make sure he calls me," Mason says. He nods at Leona and Brady and leaves.

Leona wipes her eyes and moves toward the door when Brady grabs her hand. "Hold on, wait a minute. What was that about? Are you sure you're okay?" Brady asks. "Because it looks to me like you've seen a ghost."

Leona glances at Eli and responds, "Yes, I'm fine Brady. I just feel bad for Mason is all, come on, let's go eat."

He reluctantly follows her out with a knot in the pit of his stomach. One thing he knows for sure is that Eli is not who he thought he was. He is calculating and exceptionally good at lying. *What are they hiding?*

*****

The sun is setting, but Aaron can still feel the fleeting warmth from the nature around him. The scenery is so beautiful that he can't tell where the sky ends and where the clear water beneath begins. Never in his life has he felt so overjoyed and yet so alone. Nothing makes sense, but he has relented to his surroundings and is trudging forward into a maze of green vines. His heart begins to race the longer he finds himself engrossed in this strange existence.

Near the end, he hears a noise and pauses. The sound is getting so close. He bends down and picks up a small rock. The green vines slowly fade away before his eyes.

"What brings you by?" someone whispers.

Aaron slowly turns around as the hairs on the back of his neck raise. He locks eyes with a century-old man. His brown nails are several inches long, and his grayish-white hair hangs past his shoulders. Aaron steps back, fearful that just breathing on him would break him.

"I'm Aaron."

"My name is Skrol. I expect you're wondering where you are?"

"Yes. I can't wrap my head around this place; is there a way out?" Aaron asks.

"There's always a way out, isn't there?" Skrol snorts.

Aaron looks passed Skrol and steps towards a black wrought iron gate. A giant waterfall draws him closer. He doesn't know why, but it seems to be calling him. Slow, mouthwatering whispers beckon him to come closer. He actively searches for a way in but can't find an opening.

"How do you get inside? Can you see that waterfall? I mean it's amazing," Aaron whispers.

"I think you should leave, what's inside the gate is not safe," Skrol states.

Aaron shakes his head and peers at the waterfall. He notices an enchanted existence behind the gate. *Am I dead? Is this Heaven? Why is this old man keeping me from my destiny?* he wonders.

"How do you know it's not safe? Have you been inside?" Aaron asks.

The man shakes his head no and draws the words "leave" on a single mound of dirt that has appeared out of nowhere.

Aaron rubs his eyes and blinks twice. *Why are things appearing before my eyes?* Then he figures that he must be dreaming. And if that's true, he will do everything in his power to do whatever he wants. After all, there were no limits in a dream.

"Sir, I appreciate your concern, but I am going inside that gate," Aaron declares.

Skrol stands in front of him and refuses to let him by. Aaron grits his teeth and tries to get past him, but the man is quick on his feet.

"What are you?" Aaron asks while resting his hands on his knees. He's out of breath and frustrated that this man keeps interrupting his desire.

"I'm someone who is much wiser than you. Now please go back the way you came, and you will be free," Skrol says.

Aaron contemplates Skrol's advice, but the waterfall continues calling him. He can't fight the strong pull he feels. Before realizing it, he finds himself tussling on the ground with Skrol. There is so much going on in his head it frightens him. He is desperate to get inside the gate and eager to stop a century-old fool from stopping him.

"Leave me alone!" Aaron hollers. He runs towards the gate.

Skrol tackles him and holds him down.

Aaron punches Skrol in the face, cracking the bones in his hand. "Ahh!" he screams out. He holds his hand to his chest and stares at the anomaly in front of him. He winces from the stabbing pain and lunges at Skrol.

Skrol hits Aaron with the palm of his hand, and an electric force sends Aaron flying. His body is trembling from the attack, and his legs are as limp as spaghetti. There is so much heat and pressure exuding from his face that he thinks he might combust. He sucks in a deep breath and grasps a nearby stick. He goes at Skrol with everything he has, leaving Skrol defenseless. With one last burst of energy, Aaron raises the stick in the air and aims it at Skrol's chest, but before he can make contact, Skrol disappears. The stick pierces through the ground as if it were made of butter. Aaron gets up, panting for air. He looks around, but any sign that Skrol ever existed is gone. He rubs his head, fearful of losing his mind.

Every inch of him throbs. He faces the divine existence and pauses, wondering if there really is trouble beyond the gate.

He thinks he's in over his head and that it might be best to leave, when suddenly the gate clicks and opens.

Moira

Chapter Eight

My dearest Moira,

You've been on my mind since the day I got out of the car. There is so much I wanted to say to you, but after my behavior there was nothing I could say. You deserve a great guy, someone who will cherish you forever. And I know now that that guy can't be me. I planned to live forever, but if you're reading this, then you know that I am gone. I am leaving you my entire fortune; everything I own is yours. I could think of no one else more deserving than you. You may do with it what you wish. I can only hope that I taught you well and that whatever you decide will change the world. I know you can do it. I knew the moment you first walked into Linehart Hospital that you were who I'd been waiting for. I only wish I could've given you more, but I hope this will suffice. I was born to save lives, and I know without a doubt that you were too. Please forgive me for not being the man you needed, but know that I loved you with my whole heart and soul.

Love,

Addison

Moira hunched over, almost throwing up in her mouth. She could taste the tangy residue of an orange she ate that afternoon. She glanced at Shane and carefully put the letter back in the envelope.

"I don't understand. Why would he do this?" she asked.

Shane rested his elbows on his Mahogany desk and shrugged his shoulders. He stood up, strolled over to his liquor cabinet, and retrieved two crystal glasses. Moira glanced at him and pursed her lips. Her mouth watered as he poured a splash of Crown Royal in each one and handed her a glass. She gulped it down as her mind roamed about Dr. Taylor.

For such an intelligent man, he knew practically nothing about women, she mused. *What was so hard about telling me how he felt?* The day of the meeting ran circles in her mind as she tried to contemplate his demeanor before and after he walked out of the conference room.

Shane sat on the edge of his desk in front of her and offered to refill her glass. She accepted and sipped it slowly. She looked up at him.

"May I offer you a piece of advice?" he asked.

"I'll take what I can get," she mumbled. She thought about setting the letter on fire and donating everything to charity. Her mind wandered. *Maybe we could've started something beautiful. Maybe if he'd trusted my love for him, he'd be alive today.*

Shane lifted her chin. "I've been a lawyer for fifteen years, and in that time I have witnessed quite a few calamities: you'd be surprised what family members leave their relatives. So, understand that what you're going through right now is far from weird. If there's one thing I can say about Dr. Taylor, it's that he was a man of certainty. He wouldn't have left you his fortune if he didn't trust that you would carry on his legacy and do the right thing. You'll drive yourself mad if you dwell on the *hows* and *whys,* so just focus on doing what you think is best."

She slurped the last drop of whiskey and handed him her empty glass. "I don't know what's best. I mean, there are so many zeros here," she said, slamming the papers down. "I couldn't spend this kind of money in a lifetime. And I sure as heck don't need it."

Shane scratched his head and grabbed a large yellow envelope off his desk. "Inside is a copy of his final will and testament. He didn't have any kids and since he was an only child, you shouldn't have to worry about anyone trying to contest it. You'll also find the keys to his home, mailbox, and safe," he explained.

With a long sigh, Moira lifted herself up and shoved the envelope inside of her purse.

"Thank you. I will figure this out."

Shane shook her hand. "I have no doubt," he whispered with a smile.

*****

"Dr. Moira Smith!! You have a call on line three."

The intercom yanked her away from the horrors in her head. She'd tossed and turned all night, managing to carry the stress from the day before with her. She sat down at the nearest chair and rubbed her temples as a painful band of intense numbness and tingling sensations paralyzed her. Going to work was supposed to be a distraction, but she was so replete with grief and confusion that she couldn't see straight. She grabbed her belongings and left for the day. Her heart was set on going home and crawling into bed.

The soothing drive pacified her to a point where she ceaselessly glided across the smooth road until she realized that she was pulling into Dr. Taylor's driveway. Tears flooded her eyes as she opened the envelope and took out the keys.

Stepping inside sent her nerves into a frenzy. She lost her breath, and it pained her to inhale without crying. She could feel him, smell him. He was still there. She leaned against the door, feeling annoyingly drained. The house was in disarray. Clothes, shoes, and empty food containers blanketed his living room furniture. She strolled from the door to different sections of the house, daring to get some relief as her mind garrulously ran wild with scenarios and explanations. But there was nothing she wanted—except him. It angered her that he was gone, leaving her his belongings, his money. As if she needed it. She found his study and sat behind his desk. Her tears puddled on his notes as she continued to stack books, papers, and pens into neat piles until she could actually see the desk. One thing she noticed from scanning parts of the house was that something had him very distracted.

*****

The morning sun pierced through the blinds and right into Moira's eyes. For a split second, she forgot where she was. She peeled her face from the desk and accidentally knocked over the desk phone. She picked up the receiver and somehow hit the message button.

"Hey Addison, it's Mark. Listen I thought about what you said, and I think there's a way around our dilemma. I have a friend who owes me a favor. He knows people: people willing to do anything for a little cash. Maybe we can figure something out. Call me."

She listened to the message three more times, each time feeling more and more uneasy in the pit of her stomach. She thought about calling Dr. Peters and getting an explanation, but it seemed pointless. By the time the sun set, she'd gone through countless notes and reports that Dr. Taylor did over the course of a few months. One thing she realized is that he was desperate to finish something about the brain. She opened his computer and thought of every password imaginable, but nothing worked. He entrusted her with everything, so she couldn't figure out why the passwords he used before were useless. She searched for his safe in hopes of finding some answers. The only thing inside was a thumb drive. After inserting it, she was disappointed to learn that it wasn't going to be that easy. She still needed a password. As a last ditch effort, she tried his name and then hers. Hers worked.

The screen lit up with incredibly detailed drawings and videos of his experiments. She was floored and completely blown away.

"A transmitter?" she whispered.

She spent the rest of the night watching every video he made and read every word he'd written. It was after all his last brilliant creation.

Aaron

Chapter Nine

As Mason breathes in and out, in sync with Aaron's ventilator, a strange feeling comes over him. He feels like he's burning from within and fans his face with his shirt. Blinding tears roll down his face. Appalling thoughts cross his mind, such as wishing he could have wrapped his hands around Leona's neck. He would've used his bare hands to end her life. *The same hands that touched Gisel—my angel*, he thinks.

He wonders if in some twisted way Gisel is looking out for him. Maybe it was meant to be that the police got to Leona first, before he had a chance to do the dirty work. His hands shake and perspire with such intensity that he has to run to the bathroom. He shoves his hands under the faucet and scrubs them until they are sore. The ice-cold water numbs his fingers, but he holds them there until the disturbing thoughts in his head begin to fade away.

He sits next to Aaron's bedside and takes his hand. "All this time she was...I'm sorry," he whispers. "I wish I'd known more, son."

Dr. Hopkins strolls in with a tablet and greets Mason. He goes over to the bed, takes out a small flashlight, lifts Aaron's lids and shines the light in Aaron's eyes. He performs a full examination.

"What do you think, doctor? Will my son be okay?" Mason asks.

"We won't know much until he comes out of the coma. We checked his labs, and it looks like his blood levels are not where they need to be, but they are improving. The medication we gave him to counteract the poison in his system seems to be doing its job. The brain scan came back, and it showed that he has suffered a concussion, but thankfully nothing worse than that. So far he is stable, but that doesn't mean he's out of the woods. And we have no way of knowing if there will be any lasting effects of the poison or the trauma he went through."

Mason stands up and paces the room. "I can't believe they did this to *my* son!" he grunts through gritted teeth.

"Mr. Rice, I understand your plight, but Aaron may still be able to hear you, and it's important that you stay strong for him."

"Yeah, your right, I'm sorry. I just…" He storms out of the room and in search of the nearest vending machine. He is in front of the machine jamming a dollar into the slot when he spots Brady traipsing by with a bouquet of lilies in his hand. His face pales. He bolts across the hall and slams Brady against the wall. "You did this—this is your fault!" Mason shouts.

Brady forcefully removes Mason's hands from his shirt and shoves him back. Mason stumbles into the nurse's station. He rights himself and balls his fist. He can barely catch his breath he's was so angry.

"Mason, try and calm down. I know this seems incomprehensible, but you have to know I had no idea what Leona and Eli were up to. I spent a year trying to find something to prove that she killed her ex-husband."

Mason smoothes out his clothes and steps closer. "You expect me to believe that all that time you spent with that psychopath, you never saw anything out of the ordinary?" he asks. "Even if you *thought* she killed her ex-husband, why in the hell wouldn't you get Amelia out of there? And my son— he's an innocent bystander in all this. If he dies, I'm holding you personally responsible."

"Look, I'll admit, I have seen a lot of things that seemed off. But when I say Leona is calculated and careful, that's putting it mildly. I couldn't risk blowing my cover, so I've had to be all in. It wasn't until Navid confided in me that the truth began to unfold. I'm sorry we couldn't put the pieces together sooner—for Aaron's sake—and Amelia's, and quite frankly, for everyone involved. I realize that you'd like to lash out at someone, any parent would; but the person responsible is dead."

Mason's eyes fills with tears and his bottom lip quivers. "I wish Gisel were here; she would know what to do."

Carefully placing his hand on Mason's shoulder, Brady says, "She's here with you now."

Mason nods and goes back to Aaron's room. Brady picks up the flowers off the floor and throws them in the trash. He wants to see Amelia but is so ashamed of the terrible events that have unfolded. Two teenagers are fighting for their lives, and it tears up his insides knowing that it happened right under his nose. He doesn't want Mason to know it, but he already blames himself.

*****

Aaron glances to his left, and then his right. He thinks that although Skrol is gone, somehow, another obstacle is imminent. He looks again—no one is around. He walks through the gate, and it slams shut behind him. He whirls around, startled. Now that he is on the other side, that longing need he's been feeling has drifted away with the wind.

He slips his hands in his pockets and strolls along a peony-lined path until he comes across a dark, pristine pond. He leans over and sees his reflection. He runs his fingers through his hair. The water begins to vibrate and bubble before his eyes. He steps back in fear of something flying out at him. Suddenly, he sees Amelia. He falls to his knees and stares into the water. His heart begins to pound and tears sting his eyes. He hasn't seen her in so long; it has killed him being apart from her. He sees her transform into things he never thought possible as she runs fearfully from strange creatures. He keeps his eyes peeled in fear of losing sight of her. She is in a horrific place, and he doesn't know why. *What has happened? Why isn't she with Navid and her parents*, he wonders.

"Something's wrong," he whispers. He glares into the water, afraid to look away. As he contemplates the images, he realizes that Amelia is lost, and if she's lost, then she's in more trouble than he cares to think about. He stands up and paces back and forth, trying to remember what has happened to him and why he is now in a weird dream. Amelia is apparently in a nightmare of her own. *Why?*

He sits under a nearby tree and thinks long and hard about everything that has occurred to this point when the truth practically slaps him in the face. His head shoots up; he rises and stumbles back to the pond. Tears run down his face as details of what has happened to him flood his memory. His head throbs from the remnants of that day and his worry shifts back to Amelia. "What did they do to you?!" he cries. He sees her entering a pyramid. He rubs his eyes; he is afraid for her and turns away. He looks again and sees her tearfully walking into freezing water. "Amelia—no!" he hollers.

She is completely submerged and doesn't come out.

"Oh no, I have to save her. Amelia!" he screams. He slams his fists into the water.

Amelia fades away.

He gets up and runs towards the gate. He pushes and pulls, but even with applying his own weight, he can't pry it open. He looks around and finds a large white stone and pounds on the gate over and over until the black metal starts to bend. His fingers are bleeding and his clothes are drenched in sweat. All he can think about is Amelia and how much he needs to save her. It drives him to hit the gate harder and faster.

It finally cracks open. He pushes it forward when someone touches his shoulder. He whirls around and locks eyes with a fair-skinned woman. Her slender six-foot frame is covered in a red leotard and red ballet slippers. Her fire-red hair is shaped into a spiky pixie cut.

"Hi there, I'm Bixie."

Before Aaron can respond, another woman steps from behind a freakishly perfect array of purple and red floral bushes. Her skin is pink and covered all over with raised patches that resemble burn marks. Her jet-black hair is combed into a high ponytail, and she is wearing a black leotard and a pink skirt. She bites her bottom lip and takes a bow. Her green eyes shoot up at him, and then she grins. Aaron forgets to breathe. His head is so heavy that his neck feels like a wobbling stack of pancakes.

"Don't be afraid." She steps closer. "I'm Morgan."

He hears a sound like steel sliding up against something. He turns to his left and sees a figure out of the corner of his eye; another woman is coming closer. The blood drains from Aaron's face. Her caramel skin is smooth as honey with not a single blemish. She is wearing a yellow tank top and black tights. Her golden irises penetrate into him as though she can control his every move with a look, as if he is a puppet. All he can do is stand there. His knees start to buckle, but he manages to hide it—for now. The woman is wearing a cross-body strap, which is holding something behind her back. Aaron traces the length of the object until he realizes it is a sword. A rivulet streams down his face and tickles his lips.

She opens her mouth and whispers, "I'm Helidore. But you, handsome, may call me Heli."

Aaron stares at the three women. Under normal circumstances, he would be in Heavenly bliss. But Amelia is out there somewhere, in trouble. He cannot fathom why he is here in this strange existence with three peculiar women addressing him. There is something robotic about the way they move. They glide toward the front of the gate and stand side by side.

He turns his back to them and crosses his arms. He sighs, knowing he is not going to leave by his own volition.

Moira

Chapter Ten

It was dark outside. Heavy cumulous clouds rolled in and shaded everything. It happened so quickly Moira thought for sure they would soon be at the mercy of backup generators. Whatever was happening outside didn't seem to be an ordinary rainstorm. She walked into her patient's room. With it being so dark outside, the illuminated room was blinding. The blinds in the room were open. The calamity that was about to commence would be fully exposed. Mr. Grayson sat straight up in his bed with his freckled hands clasped together. His mouth formed a hard line when he locked eyes with her. She sighed. She'd grown to read just about every facial expression a patient could muster. The fluorescent light shone down on him like a spotlight, as if he were preparing for a performance.

"So, you don't want to have the surgery?" Moira confirmed.

Mr. Grayson flashed his eyes from her to the floor like a child in trouble. He then turned his attention to the storm brewing outside the window. His light gray eyes were tired and worn, and she could just imagine the things he'd seen throughout his lifetime. She understood that this man who had to be strong his whole life was now vulnerable and afraid.

"I'm sorry Dr. Smith, I realize that this was set in motion months ago, but I honestly feel like I can wait a little longer. I'm just not ready. You know, I read that there are people out there who can will themselves to perfect health. The mind is a powerful gift. Maybe if I believe I'll get better, then just maybe I'll feel better."

Moira pulled up a chair next to his bedside and patted the back of his hand. "Mr. Grayson, I understand what you're saying. But as your doctor, I have to advise against postponing the surgery. Although the tumor is benign, it's growing at a fast rate, and if we don't remove it, it could cause a lot more pressure and damage to your brain. I realize this is unnerving at best, but please trust me, we will get it out and you can go on living a brilliant life," she explained.

Mr. Grayson nodded and agreed to sign the consent forms. Five hours later, he was in recovery. She honestly thought he would put up more of a fight. In her experience, a lot of patients can't see past their own fears and forget that she is there to save their lives.

The next day, she showed up bright and early to check on him. His wife and daughter were posted at his bedside with big smiles plastered on their faces. The sun was shining right onto Mr. Grayson's face, which seemed to set the mood for a beautiful day.

"There she is," Mr. Grayson croaked. He lifted his pale arm and pointed towards her.

Moira took his fragile hand and gave it a light shake. "How are you feeling?"

"Like a teenager. I feel like running laps around the hospital," he replied.

"Ha! Let's wait a little longer for that." She checked the surgery site and performed a quick assessment. "Everything looks good. You may have a headache for a few days, but aside from that there should be no complications. If the incision gets infected or if you have a seizure, come right back to the E.R., okay?"

"I'll make sure he's okay doctor. Thank you so much for caring and for everything you have done for him," his wife said.

"It was my pleasure," Moira replied.

Her next surgery was an hour away, and that's exactly how she wanted it. Busy days meant she was too occupied to think about Dr. Taylor's discovery. She learned so much about what he'd done that it was difficult to get it out of her head. Although she was saving lives and meeting great people like Mr. Grayson, she felt as though something was missing from her life. That euphoric feeling she used to have about going to work went away like a single breath to a match. The more she thought about his experiments, the more alive she felt, almost as if he knew this was her destiny, her purpose. He couldn't give her his love, but in her eyes, he gave her something she could live with, something she could live for. Before too long, she was practically living in his home, performing her own experiments and making more notes about the outcome. She didn't stop until she successfully created a neurotransmitter of her own.

*****

For days she didn't show up to work. Instead, she marveled at her "new baby." She was elated when her experiments worked on lab rats. However, just the fact that she could do it wasn't enough—she needed more to make her satisfied.

She worked for a month straight perfecting the device. Although she fought the urge really hard, she had to know if her transmitter worked on humans. It was a phantom itch she needed to scratch. There wasn't a scientist alive who would be satisfied with their work unless they knew it's full potential was realized. *What if her product only worked on rats?* she contemplated. It was eating her alive just wondering about it. But she knew it would be impossible to find a person who would be willing to volunteer.

One night, while drinking a glass of red wine, she dialed Dr. Peter's number. She remembered his message verbatim on Dr. Taylor's answering machine and could tell in his voice that he was intrigued. He could be the answer to her prayers.

The phone rang several times, but by the time he'd said "hello," she hung up the phone. She couldn't bear to say the words out loud—felt it was wrong. Even if he knew willing people, there was no way she could live with herself if they died because of her. She chose to let go of this obsession.

Beep! Beep! Beep! Her alarm clock blasted so loud she considered throwing it out of the window. She sat up in bed and instantly wished she hadn't. An empty bottle of wine sat on her nightstand, reminding her of last night's poor judgment. Her head pounded so hard it crippled her until she was strong enough to grab two aspirin. It was Thursday morning: one of her biggest surgery days. *No calling in sick today*, she told herself.

She made it to work almost an hour before her first procedure and hit the ground running, finishing at 5:30 p.m. As she reached into her locker for her purse, she felt every bit of her day's workload from the top of her head to the soles of her feet.

"Paging Dr. Smith," the intercom rang out.

"You've got to be kidding me," Moira griped. She threw her purse back into her locker and found the nearest elevator. She wondered why she was being paged at the end of her shift. Then she thought about Mr. Grayson and panicked. "Oh no, what if he's worse?" she whispered. She pounded on the first-floor button and ran off the elevator. Just as she headed to the nurses' station, Dr. Patel summoned her to a nearby patient who had electrodes covering her chest.

"Clear!" Nurse Ryan hollered.

The patient's body jolted up and then plopped back down like a slab of meat. Moira still found it mind-blowing how a person could be walking and talking one minute and suddenly be out cold on a gurney the next. The heart monitor pinged and a heart rate signaled the screen.

"Why was I paged Dr. Patel?" Moira asked through a yawn. She glanced at her watch and noticed it was already a quarter past six.

"I'm sorry if I worried you. It's just that you've been so busy this past year, and this is the only way I could finally meet up with you. What I'm saying is, I was hoping you would have dinner with me?"

Before she could answer the nurse yelled, "Clear!"

Moira raced over and offered her assistance. She began performing CPR as the nurse informed her of the patient's stats. When the patient was stable, Moira looked into her chart and was surprised at how many times this patient has had near-death experiences: at least four times within the past three months.

"Hey Ryan, this patient's adrenal levels are off the charts," Moira stated.

"She has Addison's Disease. She's been tolerating the treatments pretty well, but as of late she's gotten weaker and weaker. Last month she had an adrenal crisis, so we're lucky she's still with us."

Moira put the chart down and adjusted the nasal cannula in the patient's nose. The patient was a young twenty-three-year-old girl who had her whole life ahead of her. *But what quality of life will she have now?* Moira wondered. She hated moments like this when their options were limited. Maybe it was her ego, but she didn't like it when the only answer was to step aside and let things be.

"Well, she's stable for now. Thanks for helping the way you did, although it may be moot considering the situation," Nurse Ryan said.

"What do you mean?" Moira replied.

"Unfortunately, she has no one. In foster care since she was a child, dealing with this condition most of her life. Lately, she's been suicidal; you know, just wanting to end it. She stopped all treatments and now it's only a matter of time."

Moira's heart sank when she thought, *This poor child has no one who loves and cares for her.* Suddenly everything she ever complained about seemed idiotic compared to this patient's story. While the young woman was stable, Moira noticed Dr. Patel was still there, awaiting an answer. She went to him and tried to think of the best way to turn him down.

*****

The next morning, Moira bought a warehouse.

BOOK 5

"THE GATEKEEPERS OF BERYL"

BIXIE

MORGAN

HELIDORE

June 15, 1991

Bixie

Chapter Eleven

"Come on Bixie, let him go," Daina said.

"Why should I? This prick owes me fifty bucks," Bixie grunted.

Her hands were gripped tightly around Jason's impeccably starched polo shirt. As she held him inches off the ground, a moment of clarity penetrated her mind. It almost blinded her. She had absolutely no idea why she was this furious. But the one thing she knew for sure was that she was getting worse.

Jason gritted his teeth and shoved her away with his knee. He fell on his back. Bixie staggered and landed on top of Daina.

"You crazy fool," he shouted. He ran his hand across his neck. Large puffy welts had formed and his fingertips were stained with blood. His face hardened. He wanted to end her but was stopped by a rancid wave of rotting trash. The contents in a nearby dumpster suffocated him and rattled his stomach until he was bent over and heaving.

Daina put both hands on Bixie's face and wiggled her shoulders. "Stay with me Bix, we need to get you to a hospital."

Bixie shook her head. Although she felt as though she was shutting down like a toy with dying battery, her answer was no. She broke out into a sweat. Her body had once again retaliated against her. Keeping her eyes open was a struggle, until she relented into a painful abyss of her deepest memories.

*****

"Why can't I stay with you? You said you loved me," Bixie cried.

"I do love you, that's why you have to go with Ms. Stafford. She's going to take you to a safer place," her mother said.

Bixie ran to the bathroom and locked the door. "I'm never coming out," she shouted, defiantly.

Her mother planted her face in her hands and sobbed. Ms. Stafford handed her a tissue and gently stroked her hand. "I'll make sure she's in a good home."

"I'm putting my seven-year-old daughter's life in your hands. You *have* to make sure she's always safe. And please, don't ever tell her about my condition. She can never know that I'm sick."

"You have my word. Bixie will always be in good care. But I'd be remiss if I didn't ask you one last time to reconsider your decision. There has to be another way than dying alone. Maybe we can figure something out," Ms. Stafford pleaded.

"No, I've thought really hard about this. There is nothing more that can be done about my condition, so I'm choosing to live out the rest of my days in this highly recommended hospice facility."

Ms. Stafford wanted desperately to interject but opted against it.

"Believe me, if there were any other way, I would've done it. I want Bixie to remember me like this, not withering away into nothing."

By the time the sun set, young Bixie had said her goodbyes and was escorted to a local facility until Ms. Stafford could legally adopt her.

Shortly after her ninth birthday, Ms. Stafford was killed in a car accident, leaving Bixie once again in the care of the state. Over the years, Bixie grew to realize that her mother was never coming back and that she was all alone in the world—until she met Daina. They met in foster care as teenagers and remained close friends ever since. When they turned eighteen, they got jobs and an apartment together. Life was bearable until Bixie was diagnosed with Addison's disease. With her being sick all the time it began to put a strain on their friendship, and Bixie hated herself for being a burden to her only friend. So, she decided to do something about it.

*****

"She's crazy, I can't believe you're coddling her after that," Jason complained.

Daina glared at him and dragged Bixie to the car. Jason hopped into the driver's seat and started the engine.

"So, you're not going to help me?" Daina asked while shoving Bixie's feet inside.

"Hell no! She's lucky I don't leave her on the side of the road. Speaking of which, I say we drop her off at the looney bin."

Daina slammed the car door shut and slumped down in the passenger's seat. Tears pooled her eyes when they drove off. She'd had the perfect birthday: great food and margaritas from her favorite Mexican restaurant with her two favorite people. But now her perfect day was ruined, and she couldn't shake this terrible feeling in the pit of her stomach. She sniffed deeply to keep the tears from rolling as she stared out the window.

Jason reached over and slid his hand into hers. He brought it to his lips. "I'm sorry, babe. I could've handled that better."

"Yes, you could have. You know she can't control herself when she gets angry. Taunting her was not smart. But I do understand how you feel," she replied.

"Do you? Because sometimes I feel like you choose her over me, and I hate it," Jason said.

"I don't choose her over you. It's just that she's like a sister to me, and I feel like I have to protect her. She can't help that she's always sick."

"I know that, but it's not your responsibility to drop everything for her. It's not fair to you, or us."

"I can't lose her Jason. She's tried to end her life because she hates being a burden. I don't know how long I'll have her because her illness could take her out or she may try to end it again. I won't ever give up on her, and I hope you'll always be by my side no matter what happens."

"Of course I'll always be by your side. I just worry about you is all." Jason looked straight ahead and smiled.

"Seriously? What could possibly make you smile at a time like this?" Daina asked.

"I was just thinking about that stupid bet she and I made. Remind me to never make a bet with her again."

Daina giggled. "Well, you do owe her fifty bucks. Who knew that guy would fall off the bull," she whispered through a laugh.

While Bixie was still unconscious, they pulled up to Riverleaf Hospital.

"What are you doing? She doesn't want to be at the hospital," Daina said.

"It's not up to her. She could die, Daina. We wouldn't be good friends to her if we just take her home without getting her proper medical care."

Daina bit her bottom lip. She was shaking with fear but knew he was right. Before she knew it, the medical team was running out with a gurney and proceeded to hook Bixie up to an IV. Daina kissed Bixie on the forehead and whispered, "I'll see you soon, sis."

Daina and Jason headed home, exhausted from the day. Jason promised they would check on Bixie in the morning. When Daina awoke in the middle of the night from a nightmare, she made several calls to the hospital until she was told by a nurse that Bixie had passed away.

*****

Bixie opened her eyes and could not make out where she was. Machines were going on and off, and a bright fluorescent light was above her head. She pulled out an IV from her right arm and tried to sit up, but her body was too heavy. She wiggled her feet and was relieved that she wasn't paralyzed; she felt as though she had died. Suddenly, she heard footsteps clacking against the linoleum floor. A woman appeared in her line of vision. Bixie looked up at her in fear.

"Hello, Bixie. I'm Dr. Moira Smith."

October 30, 1991

Morgan

Chapter Twelve

It was Halloween eve, Morgan's favorite time of the year. Normally, she would be planning her annual costume party...but not this year. From the moment she opened her eyes this morning she was reminded of her lousy breakup with Roy and was in no mood to celebrate anything. Instead, she quietly strolled throughout her best friend's cabin and admired the décor. Lindsay was always a lifesaver in her time of need. She paused at a floor-to-ceiling window and looked out as the sunrise touched each and every leaf on a nearby tree. But even the sun wasn't hot enough to warm her spirit. She was perpetually cold the moment she ended things with Roy. And the sneaky, cool breeze slipping through the window from across the room wasn't helping. She slammed it shut and secured the latch.

After brewing a hot cup of chamomile tea, she scanned the bookshelf for a great read and settled on an old favorite. A book of O. Henry short stories piqued her interest. Page after page, she was happily submerged into literary bliss until a wrap at the door extracted her from her escape. She wasn't expecting any company and was positive no one knew of her whereabouts. When they knocked again, she slammed the book shut and peeked out the window.

"Who's there?" she whispered.

The person on the other side banged again, this time harder and with more force. She quietly unlocked the door and opened it just enough to poke her head out. She glanced to her left and right and closed it abruptly. Now she was spooked. She'd made the mistake of watching a marathon of horror movies last night, and now her skin was crawling. She tiptoed to the kitchen and pulled out a butcher knife from Lindsay's *Pampered Chef* collection. Then she put it back, knowing Lindsey would kill her if she scuffed up her precious kitchen cutlery, even if it was for a good cause. A large hammer hung on the wall next to the back door.

By the time Morgan got a good grip around the tool, a rock had flown through the window and barely missed her head. She screamed so loud her throat constricted, yet she couldn't hear a sound. Her hands and feet tingled in retaliation as her nerves ran wild. Little specs of glass covered her feet. There was no escape. She ran to the bathroom, making a trail of bloody footprints along the way and locked the door. With her heart pounding and her hand shaking, she bent down and pulled out a small shard of glass from her foot. A bloody rivulet seeped out of the opening. It took her an abundance of concentration not to faint, but she managed to keep her eyes open. She slid into the bathtub and brought her knees to her chest.

A large thump from beyond the door made her heart pound harder. She had never been so frightened in her life. Sweat droplets bubbled on her forehead and hands, but she was determined that she was not going to die without a fight. She squeezed her eyes shut as the person's shoes crunched through the glass and stopped outside the bathroom door. Morgan held her breath and waited for whoever was brazen enough to enter. She heard heavy breathing and puffing for air. *Is he out of shape*, she wondered. She quietly rose up and tried desperately to ignore the sharp, stabbing pain from the cuts on her feet. It was now or never. She put her hand on the doorknob and twisted it.

The person kicked the door open and knocked Morgan down. She hit her head on the sink and landed on her side. The hammer flew out of her hands and slammed against the toilet with a thud. She opened her eyes and saw two of everything. With visions of objects clouding her eyesight, she felt around for the hammer and finally found it when the man stomped on her hand. She cried out from the pain and was sure a few of her fingers were broken.

"Please leave me alone," she begged as she faded in and out of consciousness.

"I was hired by your ex," the stranger said. He reached down and wrapped his massive hands around her throat and squeezed.

"Ahh! No please stop," Morgan pleaded.

*****

"Morgan wake up! You're safe," Colton said as he rubbed the side of her face.

"No, no, please leave me alone!" she screamed. She opened her eyes and locked eyes with him. A sense of relief came over her. His calm baby blue eyes were her home. "It was just a dream," she said as the nurse rushed in. Morgan's heart monitor went into a beeping frenzy. She felt a chill come over her as soon as Colton's warm hand slipped away. Her chest was heavy, and she was sick and tired of the crushing sensation and of always trying to catch her breath. She just couldn't get enough air, no matter how hard she tried.

Colton stepped aside and wiped tears from his eyes. He and Morgan locked eyes and stayed in a loving trance until hers closed. He was escorted out of the room and froze right outside the door. He slumped down and buried his face in his hands. An entire medical team raced into the room, carrying tubes and a crash cart. He heard every word of medical jargon that escaped their lips and still had no earthly idea what they were saying. But he knew without a doubt that those foreign words were used time and time again to save Morgan's life.

He'd prayed once before when he almost lost her. He had prayed for more time. God had answered his prayers. Morgan lived longer than anyone ever expected, even though her heart and lungs were surrounded by scar tissue. Within that year her life was spared, and pieces of his life slowly disappeared. He selfishly wanted more and more time but knew that Morgan was tired and only living for him. He realized that his prayer may not be her prayer; what's good for him may not be good for her. So this time, he pulled himself off the floor and went to the chapel.

It was surreal, being that this might be his last time there, asking yet again for something. *How many times have I made promises to God to plead for what I've wanted?* he mused. He sat on the second to last row, took a deep breath, and prayed. He didn't ask for more time with her. Instead, he asked for strength and for Morgan to be at peace.

By the time he walked out into the hallway, he knew his love was gone. His heart suddenly felt empty, and a cold draft made him shiver. Tears pooled in his eyes as the nurses sorrowfully stared at him. But he pushed forward and took the most difficult walk of his life. He passed by several rooms where there was still life and people's lives were being saved. His last step was inside Morgan's room, where death had come and gone, taking his beloved with him.

He sat on the edge of her bed and kissed her hands—one finger at a time.

"Sleep well, my love," he whispered. He looked away and, in his grief, broke down into tears.

"Ugh!" Morgan croaked.

Colton jumped back in shock and pressed himself against the wall. Then, he ran out of the room shouting, "She's still alive! Nurse!"

The nurses rushed in and stopped at the door. For seconds it seemed as though everything and everyone was frozen in time. When the shock wore off, the nurses went to work. Morgan had once again flat-lined, and they brought her back again. Colton was taking it all in from an unknown vantage point to him—as if he'd left his body. He had no control and couldn't move if he wanted to. They shoved a tube down her throat and turned on a breathing machine. Dr. Moser patted Colton on the shoulder, breaking him out of a distant place and walked him just outside the door.

"Mr. Galvin, I'm afraid there's not much more we can do for Morgan. Given the complications from her Scleroderma condition, at this point, we can only keep her alive by machine. What happened earlier has never happened in this hospital before. The fact that she came back for a short period was a miracle, even if it was short-lived." Dr. Moser paused. "Do you have any questions for me?" he asked.

"I—I just don't understand how that could happen. I mean, she was gone…and then she came back. Are you sure there is nothing you can do? Maybe some experiment or medical trial? You said yourself, that's never happened before."

"I'm afraid we've used every resource imaginable, Mr. Galvin."

"All I know is that for the past year, she's had nightmares about someone attacking her, and each time she wakes up it takes a toll on her heart. I just want her to be at peace, and I feel that there has to be something we can do," Colton declared.

"I understand what you're saying, and I wish there was more we could do. It's painful to see a patient so young go through something like this, but all we can do is accept the hand we're dealt and make the most of it. Cherish your time with her Mr. Galvin. She may still be able to hear your voice, and if that's true, maybe she will go in peace," Dr. Moser said.

Colton followed the doctor's advice. For the next three days, he read to Morgan some of her favorite romance novels and reminisced about some of their funniest moments together. He hoped that his stories reached her and she would rest in peace. On the fourth day, he expressed how much he loved her and would never forget her. He gave her one last kiss and turned off the machine. After three of the longest minutes of his life, Morgan took her final breath.

*****

Morgan could hear the final words from her love as she ran through a beautiful green field of red and purple flowers. She was happy and excited to see whatever dreams were on the horizon. Suddenly, she heard a woman's voice: one she'd never heard before. She opened her eyes and took in a deep breath, and then another. She was surprised that it wasn't painful; she could expand her lungs for the first time in years without feeling like she was inside a box. Her heart thumped at a normal pace, and her chest didn't feel like someone was sitting on it. *What's happening?* she wondered.

"Am I alive?" she asked the woman.

"Yes, sweetheart. You are alive." The woman held out her hand.

Morgan sat up and looked around. "Who are you?"

"I'm Dr. Moira Smith."

May 8, 1992

Baltimore, MD

Helidore

Chapter Thirteen

"Remember, if you don't win this fight you're finished. No one is going to sponsor a nobody. Now I know you can fight because I trained you myself. So you must give it one hundred and ten percent. This is your last chance to prove to the world that you are a star and that you are not just good, but great. We've gotten you this far, the rest is up to you."

Helidore remembered her trainer's so-called "pep-talk" verbatim and tried to cram any negative thoughts into the furthest corners of her mind. He was always straight forward with her, which she appreciated. But now was not the time to add on more pressure.

She was fifteen when she'd met Jim. Before that, she lived wherever she could lay her head. He took her under his wing and did the best he could. He made sure she had a place to go and food to eat, and never asked anything of her in return. It wasn't long before he brought her to his gym. She was mesmerized and fell in love with the smell, the pain, and the misery of vigorous training. She knew she could handle whatever bumps and bruises came with the territory.

Initially, Jim wanted her to pass out towels, but he quickly learned that Helidore was a fighter. She was in her element and started to feel like she mattered. The gym was a respite, but sometimes she fought hard to ignore the strong pull of being on the streets—it would be so easy to go back to them. But luckily for her, Jim cared more about her well-being than she ever could. The more she trained, the better boxer she became. She sparred and competed a lot; her passion was to be an MMA fighter, which Jim fully supported.

"Helidore Stevens!" The announcer shouted, startling her. She hadn't noticed him stepping into the ring. He was donned in a three-piece navy blue suit and wreaked of ridiculously strong cologne. Her nose burned from the fumes. He gripped the microphone and congratulated her for her courage. Before she knew it, her opponent, Greta Monee, was making her way out of the tunnel. Loud music boomed throughout the auditorium, and the crowd went into a maniacal frenzy over their prized fighter. They were adorned in her colors of purple, red, and silver. Helidore couldn't tell where one person began and the other ended. She wondered just how disappointed they were about to be when she annihilated their undefeated treasure. *Would they cheer for the new champion?* she wondered.

She stretched and moved around the ring in a clockwise motion, warming up. While doing so, she felt a small tinge of disappointment that there was no one there to cheer her on. No friendly faces in the crowd, just a mass of decorated madness. Nonetheless, she slid her mouthpiece between her teeth and bit down, hard.

The bell sounded, and Helidore sprang into action.

She slipped a jab that rocked Greta's head back. Greta kicked Helidore in the knee, but she recovered quickly. She was light on her feet as she moved about the ring, throwing jabs and landing powerful kicks throughout the fight.

She landed a good shot in Greta's jaw, but her opponent didn't seem fazed by it. She punched her again and swept her leg. Greta stumbled back but was still tough and bounced back onto her feet. Helidore knew it was time for a takedown, so she hit Greta in the stomach and grabbed her by the shoulders. Greta bent over and gasped for air. Helidore pinned Greta's arm behind her back and took her down.

Helidore glanced at her trainer, who was screaming obscenities from the side of the ring. By the time she made out what he was saying, Greta had somehow gotten out of the stronghold and repeatedly punched Helidore in the face. She recovered quickly and kicked Greta hard. The bell rang again. They went to their corners and were thoroughly berated by their trainers. Helidore rolled her eyes and hoped that the bell would ring soon. She would rather take repeated hits to the face than sit another second listening to Jim complain about her performance.

Rounds two and three went by so quickly Helidore wasn't sure who won them. She was tired. She'd never had to fight past the third round. She always trained hard no matter who she was up against, but right now she felt as if she'd underestimated Greta's talent. Jim squirted cool water in her mouth while he gave her advice for the final round. The bell rang and she was back on her feet and ready to end it.

She moved around the ring, gaining one last burst of energy before going in for the final takedown. There was a minute left when Helidore punched Greta and swept her leg. This time Helidore knew that Greta was tired as she fell back. Helidore jumped on her and locked Greta's arm in a hold. She kept pulling and pulling and had every intention on breaking it until Greta finally tapped out. Only seconds were left on the clock when the referee ended the fight. Helidore was beside herself. She ran to her trainer and jumped into his arms. There was pride in his eyes, and it made her emotional. For so long she never really knew what it felt like to be loved, and this moment was proof of all she had ever wanted. It wasn't about winning, but about perseverance. She fought hard and overcame so much, and Jim was truly happy for her.

As she made her way out of the ring, the crowd cheered. She looked back at Greta who was now being examined by a physician.

"They're cheering for you Helidore," Jim said, proudly.

She stared back at them and held up her belt, waving it around.

"Helidore! Helidore! Helidore!" they roared.

There was nothing that could tear her away from the high. News reporters and media personnel had cameras in her face, taking pictures and asking questions. She reveled in it. All of the hard work she endured had paid off, and she intended to enjoy her life to the fullest.

*****

The following morning she awoke with a start. Her winning belt was right next to her, reminding her of last night's victory. It was real. She smiled and rubbed the gold medal on the front, and sniffed the smooth black leather.

After making a fresh pot of coffee, she headed to the gym for her daily morning workout. Even with her win, she still wanted to stay sharp and in shape. To her surprise, Jim wasn't there, so she unlocked the doors and turned on all the lights. Her stomach was in knots when she thought about her upcoming interview that afternoon. She warmed up and decided to do weight training. She was on her third set when she heard footsteps. She glanced at the clock: 7:30 AM.

"Jim? Is that you?" she grunted while lifting. No one answered back. She kept lifting, staying focused because no one was there to spot her. She was finishing her final lift when someone pushed down on the weight. She panicked and struggled to get free. One hundred pounds was pressed across her chest. She was trapped.

"Hey, what the hell are you doing?" she sputtered. Her eyes focused on a man, one that was part of her past. Someone she hoped to never see in her future. "Byron? What do you want?"

"You owe me," he said through gritted teeth. "You thought I would forget that you stole from me?"

"I was a child back then. I needed the money, I was starving," she explained.

"No one steals from me," he groaned and pressed the weight closer to her neck.

"Please, I—I can get you the money. It was...fifty bucks, right?" she struggled to force the words out.

"No, you owe me more than that. You're big time now. That fifty bucks comes with interest, and maybe a few connections. The way I see it, you owe me until I say you're paid in full."

"What! You can't do that. Look, I'll pay you the fifty I took, plus an extra thousand. How's that?" Helidore asked. Tears formed in her eyes. She was suddenly fifteen years old again and at the mercy of people who were worse than dirt. She got away from that life, but that life didn't get away from her. "Byron please...let me go."

"Alright, alright. I'll let you go," he whispered and lifted the bar a few inches.

Helidore rushed from under the weight and stood a few steps back from him. She wiped her eyes on a gym towel. She was thinking about beating the crap out of him when she heard another set of footsteps. It was Donna.

"Surely, you didn't think it would be that easy." Donna said.

Helidore couldn't believe her eyes. The closest thing she had to a childhood friend was this grown woman standing there now wearing expensive clothing and jewelry. But in their lifestyle, that could only mean one thing.

"Donna, don't tell me you're working with this sleaze. We talked about getting away from him and his influence," Helidore stated.

"Like you care. You left and never came back. Don't pretend like you gave me a second thought after your new life. Now you're miss big-shot fighter with a career."

"We can work together. I can help you if you would let me."

"It's too late for that. I'm not someone you need to feel sorry for!" she screamed. She picked up a free weight and lunged for Helidore. They fell to the ground. Helidore slapped Donna and kicked her a few feet away. Byron grabbed Helidore and hit her in the head with the weight.

She was fluttering between reality and fantasy. Nothing made sense until she opened her eyes.

*****

"Oh my word, you're a miracle worker. She was brain dead," Dr. Patel stated.

"The transmitter worked again. I wasn't sure we could pull this off a third time, but luckily your medical conference in Maryland was the trip of a lifetime. Who knew you would stumble upon another viable person?" Dr. Moira Smith gave him a kiss on the cheek and turned her attention to Helidore.

"Helidore, I'm Dr. Moira Smith, and this is my colleague Dr. Patel. How do you feel, dear?"

BOOK 6

"AMELIA"

Amelia

Chapter Fourteen

Sharon stumbled and fell forward. Her hands were still tightly gripped at the bottom edge of Navid's shirt and were slipping. He was intractable and practically dragging her across Amelia's hospital room. They knew it was a possibility that Amelia wouldn't make it, but living in the moment of this calamity was just as catastrophic as she imagined. A world with no Amelia was a world with no sunshine. The nurses were taking turns performing CPR, and then one of them stuck a needle in her IV, but the monitor still flat-lined. Navid was inches away from grabbing Amelia's hand before a nurse escorted him out of the room.

"They have to save her, Sharon. They can't give up on her!" he cried.

"She will make it my love. She has to," Sharon replied.

They were both trembling with overwhelming fright. Sharon buried her face in her hands and tried hard to stifle a wail. She lifted her head and wondered if Alexandria had any idea that her daughter was lying in a hospital bed, fighting for her life. She peered through the small window in the door and prayed that they could restart Amelia's heart.

*****

Amelia couldn't believe her eyes. In all her life, there was no greater feeling than living in this time and in this moment. Ever since Gisel had revealed everything to her, she wasn't sure if it was possible to really understand the importance of life and how precious it really is. She was given a second chance, but wondered, *What if I don't want it?* She understood that it would be easier to stay here with him and live out all eternity in happiness. *Who wouldn't choose that?* she mused. Until now, she had no idea he existed and that all of this time he was protecting her, rooting for her, and loving her in the most innocent way possible. Nothing could be more beautiful than that. *Maybe being here has been my destiny all along*, she thought.

"It's time for you to go," he said. Almost as if he heard her thoughts.

Her heart fluttered. Even when he spoke, it sounded like a song. *Everyone sounds like a melody here*, she observed. *How can I leave someone I just met, who it happens, has known me my whole life?* She crossed her arms and furrowed her brow, contemplating her options.

"There is nothing for you to decide. It's time," he stated.

"I thought it was my choice to do whatever I wanted," Amelia replied.

"Oh, it is. Until you decide wrong," he said through a laugh. He took her hand and walked her over to a golden bridge.

"There's no such thing as a wrong choice in Heaven."

"True, but you and I both know that you don't belong here until you have lived a long and happy life," he whispered.

"I—I'm happy now," she declared. "Going back is just so hard. Because no matter which road I choose, I don't know if it's the right one. I don't know what will happen."

"Not knowing what will happen is what makes it beautiful. Choices are a gift. Life is full of endless roads and tunnels; sometimes you have to walk, and sometimes you have to crawl. But no matter what you choose, you're strong enough to handle it."

Amelia rolled her eyes and held out her arms for a hug, knowing he was right. "I'm so glad we met. I will never forget you. Can't wait to see you again...Andrew."

"That's going to take some getting used to. But I will miss you, Amelia, very much," he said and smiled.

She said her final goodbyes and slowly walked over the golden-plated bridge. She never wanted to forget the way the smooth railing felt under her fingertips as they slowly disappeared. Or the way her hair swept in the silk breeze. By the time her foot reached the soft grass on the other end, she looked back, and Andrew was gone. With a sigh, she mounted Asa alongside Anthony. She waved goodbye to Anita.

"We're going to miss you, you know," Anthony whispered.

"I'm going to miss you all, too."

Asa lifted up and glided through the sky so gracefully that it took Amelia a second to realize they were flying. She held tight and marveled at the colorful scenery beneath them and the beautiful trees adorned with delicious fruit. Her heart almost stopped as she remembered the taste of only a few. *There will never be water as blue and air as clean*, she thought. *Nothing compares and nothing ever will.* Every tangible thing in her grasp slowly slipped away, and she knew that had to be okay. Still, she couldn't hold back the tears—they rolled down her face and dried, as if someone was kissing them away. She looked ahead as Asa's indelible wings flew them towards the sun.

*****

"We're going to have to call it. She's not coming back," Nurse Sheldon stated. She wanted to break down. How many lives had she saved, and lost? It came with the job. But this time there was a terrible feeling in the pit of her stomach. She ran every method they tried over and over in her head to see if they missed something. Amelia's body temperature kept dropping no matter what they did, and they never stopped doing CPR. The medical team was still trying everything they could to bring her back, but nothing was working. Her body was already weak, and there wasn't much more to be done.

Dr. Wallis somberly checked his watch. The medical team carefully removed their hands from Amelia and stepped away. It was as if a funeral had commenced. Every head was bowed. Hands were clasped together.

"Time of death…"

"No! Don't you call it," Navid screamed through the door. He pushed it open and was apprehended by two nurses. Amelia was pale. He knew there wasn't much time. He forcefully ran to her bedside and grabbed her by the shoulders and shook her. Her limp body flopped against the bed. "Come on Amelia. You promised you would come back. Breathe!" He kept shaking her and rubbing her arms. "One more time Doc, please," he whispered.

"Navid, I'm sorry, but she's gone," Dr. Wallis stated.

Navid shook his head no. "She's not! I know her. She'll come back. Just one more time. Please!"

Dr. Wallis glanced at his team. They were all too eager to try again. Nurse Sheldon couldn't shake the feeling that it wasn't over. She even felt relieved to continue. She ordered the staff to bring warm blankets as they went back to work on Amelia. Dr. Wallis inserted something in her IV. Navid hadn't expected them to listen to him, but he stood back and watched and waited. The heart monitor was still flat-lined.

"Come on Amelia. The rest is up to you. Fight dammit!" Navid shouted.

"Oh my word...we have a pulse," Nurse Sheldon cheered.

Navid's trembling knees buckled as he collapsed to the floor.

Aaron

Chapter Fifteen

Aaron stares into Amelia's deep blue eyes and wonders if she could possibly be any more beautiful. He caresses her face, and the warmth of her cheeks is all that convinces him that she isn't a figment of his imagination. They are lying under a cherry tree, which is brimming with stunning flowers. When the wind blows, pink flurries blanket them and tickle their skin. Amelia whispers her deepest secrets and her wildest dreams, and he is entranced with every word she utters. She scoots closer to him and rests her head on his chest while he runs his fingers through her silken hair.

They are as close as humanly possible, but he still worries that this love could slip through his fingers. Every time he feels happy, his mind races to dark places that he can't escape.

He shakes with anxiety but calms when she begins humming a song he's never heard before. His racing heart slows down. And his body temperature cools one degree at a time. Amelia is his balance on an uncalibrated scale.

When the humming stops and the sweet breeze disappears, Aaron opens his eyes. He sits up and curses his reality. Amelia is out there somewhere, and he has no idea how to get to her. But he has to try.

He runs towards the gate and shoves Helidore out of the way. She barely moves an inch, as if she were made of solid rock. He glares at her and grits his teeth.

"Get out of my way." With a single push of a finger, she shoves him ten feet away.

"Ahh!" he hollers and lands in a bush. Razor sharp thorns pierce his arms as he crawls his way out. He marches back over to the three women and says, "I have to go. Someone I love is in danger; if I don't save her, she could die."

Bixie, Morgan, and Helidore glance at each other and giggle loudly.

Aaron thinks they are repulsive. His face turns red and the hairs on the back of his neck rise. He lunges at Bixie and immediately regrets it as his body recoils from the heat. Barely touching her causes his whole body to feel like it is on fire. The heat will not subside no matter what he does. He feels like he's being bathed in lava. He runs to a nearby pond and dunks his entire body in until the intensifying heat subsides. He leaps out of the ice-cold water and rests in the grass, panting and coughing…praying for air.

As soon as his body has cooled, he hears a raucous noise and follows the sound to an opening. The three of them are sitting, mocking him and laughing at his misery. They snack on purple berries and remain utterly oblivious to him. He steps back and realizes that they are not guarding the gate. He runs as fast and hard as he can and reaches for the lever when Morgan lands directly in front of him. He balls his fist and punches her in the face.

"Ahh!" he screams in agony. He hunches over and holds his hand tight against his body, but the pain only gets worse. He dares to look at it and falls to his knees. Every bone in his hand is broken. Hitting her was parallel to hitting a rock. Helidore and Bixie stand next to Morgan and cross their arms in sync.

"Why is this happening?" he grunts.

"We were given orders to guard the gate, and to never let a single soul escape," Bixie replies.

"What are you? Who made you like this?" He stares at the three of them, unable to understand why they were even created.

Helidore looks at the girls and asks, "Should we tell him?"

Morgan and Bixie nod.

Helidore kneels down, looks Aaron in the eyes and says, "Years ago, we were created by a doctor who wanted to give us a second chance at life. Each of us experienced terrible things that we could not come back from under normal circumstances. She's a brilliant scientist who created life within us and made us all unique."

She points at Bixie and continues, "Her adrenaline levels were amplified to the point that she has the power to burn you alive with a single touch." She turns to Morgan. "Morgan had Scleroderma, so her skin was designed to be impenetrable. No matter what you do, you can't pierce her skin because it's harder than rock."

She stands up and says, "And then there's me. I was a great fighter, stronger than anyone I knew. But I had a terrible past that came back to haunt me. I was hit in the head and would've died until a miracle happened. She increased my strength, and here we are."

Aaron can't believe his ears. "How old are you? Why has no one ever heard of you?"

"We keep a low profile. We only come out at night. We have fought criminals for years, and no one ever suspected us until a few years ago. The government got word of our existence, so our liberator had to hide us and put us on ice. We've been here ever since."

"Look, I'm no criminal. It's okay to let me go," Aaron pleads.

"No. You have to die. No one can ever know about us, and you already know everything. We can't take any chances," Helidore says.

"I promise not to say anything. I mean, this is absurd. I don't even know if I'm alive or dead. So I can't imagine you being any safer than that."

Morgan giggles. "Oh, sweet little soul. If you're alive and wake up, then you can tell the world and expose us. And if you're dead, you can let other souls know about us, and then we'll have hell trying to keep them out of our safe place," Morgan explains.

"Then why did you tell me?" he implores.

The three keep laughing at him.

"You know what I think? I think you girls are evil and enjoy other's misery. Something about your creation goes against humanity, and you should all be dead. Otherwise, if it were such a miracle, then everyone would know about you. And that doctor should be in jail!" he yells, livid.

Blinded by his anger, Aaron does not notice them getting closer and closer to him. He backs himself against a tree. There is nowhere to go. Helidore reaches behind her back and pulls out a sword so large that he can see his reflection in the metal. She raises it in the air. Aaron squeezes his eyes shut.

Click! They all hear the lock to the gate open.

*****

Anthony gives Amelia one last burst of power. Instead of saying goodbye, she winks at him and strolls forward. Her heart starts beating again, strong and powerful. She stands in the shadows as her mind races about Joleus and his bright blue eyes and blond hair. She is aware that making choices is terribly hard and confusing, but she has made hers and will not regret one second of it. Whatever power she has been given, it makes her light on her feet. Her adrenaline is rushing through her veins like fire to a line of kerosene. She pushes the gate open and walks through.

No one is around.

She saunters forward and stops at the large waterfall. It is just as hypnotic as she dreamed before. The sound, the smell of fresh water, and even the taste as it sprayed onto her lips is all familiar.

"Who are you?" Bixie asks.

Amelia whirls around and locks eyes with a woman—red like a firecracker from head to toe. Amelia crosses her arms and steps closer. Two more women join the red woman and stop just a few feet away from her.

"I'm Amelia, and you are?"

Each of the women's eyes shift back and forth. They seem puzzled about something.

Helidore points to each of the girls and says, "This is Bixie and Morgan. I'm Helidore."

"I was looking for someone named Aaron. Have you seen him?"

"No," Bixie blurts out.

Amelia cocks her head to one side. "Now Bixie, you wouldn't be lying to me now would you?"

Bixie purses her lips. Helidore rolls her eyes and whispers, "Amelia, how would you like to hear our story? I'm sure you're wondering about us and why we're here."

"No, I'm good. I just want to find Aaron," she replies.

Bixie walks closer and huffs, "I think our friend here needs to be taught some manners." She touches Amelia's arm.

"Ouch!" Amelia tries to rub the pain away but it won't subside. She closes her eyes and concentrates on the area; the searing heat slowly fades away. She opens her eyes and kicks Bixie in the stomach.

Bixie winces from the shocking pain, but quickly recovers. She reaches for Amelia's neck, but Amelia moves back and picks up a large rock. Morgan and Helidore are beyond words as they stare. Amelia throws the rock at Bixie.

Morgan blocks it and shatters it into rubble.

"No! This is my fight," Bixie yells at Morgan.

"Fine," Morgan says and strides a few feet away with Helidore.

Bixie gains purchase from the grass and jumps on Amelia. Amelia's entire body is on fire, and there is no amount of concentration that can save her from the debilitating pain. But she has to find a way to suffer through it as she fights for her life. She puts both hands on each side of Bixie's face and squeezes.

Bixie can't get her head free as Amelia keeps tightening the pressure. They end up rolling down a hill and land in front of a pond.

Amelia channels the last bit of energy, and with all her strength, throws Bixie into the water.

August 12, 2017

Moira

Chapter Sixteen

Moira sashayed into her new lab and inhaled the fresh paint. It was the smell of victory. There was no way the government would find them in her brand new underground lab. She was on top of the world and was enamored with herself. There was not a single person alive who could do what she had done in the amount of time she did it. She pushed open a side door and followed the winding steps into a basement that led her to her secret weapons. She marveled at the three women who were sleeping peacefully in their pods. She checked their vitals and heart monitors and connected any loose wiring. After that, she synchronized her watch with their monitors so that even when she was away, she would know if they were okay. They had already done great things together and would continue to perform miracles. She wanted an army of girls—women— and was well on her way to finding more prospects. But she couldn't do it alone. She walked into her operating room and wrapped her arms around her love.

"Back so soon, beautiful?" Dr. Patel said as he turned around and kissed her.

She stared into his eyes and melted. There was something powerful and sinister about him, and she admired it. She never thought she could love someone as much as she loved Dr. Taylor. And if it wasn't for Dr. Patel's persistence, she would've never known what a great partner he would be.

*****

It was the night she revived Bixie. She had secretly transferred the young girl to her brand new warehouse, which was located on the outskirts of town. Moira convinced herself that she was doing the right thing. She knew that no one would miss Bixie; after all, she had no family and from what she gathered, no friends to make a big fuss over her whereabouts. She paid her friend Nurse Melody to tell everyone that Bixie had died.

Everything was in place for her to perform the surgery. She spared no expense and purchased the best lighting and medical equipment that money could buy. For the first time she was happy Dr. Taylor left her so much money. She was desperate to see if her creation worked and hoped she wasn't wasting her time. After donning scrubs and her surgical mask, she assiduously scrubbed her arms and hands for ten minutes until they were raw. Inside of the operating room, there were two long trays with sterile instruments spread out evenly and a pair of sterile gloves waiting for her insured hands to perform a miracle. Her nerves were all over the place and her armpits perspired, but luckily for her, her hands were never shaky during her surgeries.

She took a deep breath and carefully acquired the scalpel. The neurotransmitter was implanted in the occipital lobe. Since it was responsible for vision, she figured it would be the best telltale once Bixie opened her eyes. It took her two hours from implantation to suturing Bixie closed. Now all she could do was wait and hope it worked, since there were no apparent complications.

Hours and hours went by—still no change. Moira was devastated. It appeared that Bixie was only being kept alive by the machine she was hooked up to. She walked in and out of the operating room, each time hoping Bixie would wake up. After scrubbing her hands for the third time and washing all of the equipment she'd used, she thought about all of the hard work she put into this creation and slammed a tray against the wall.

"Crap!" she screamed.

She rushed to the wall and was about to unplug Bixie's machine when she heard a sound. She picked up her scalpel and left the operating room. The noise was coming from the lab. Her heart pounded against her chest. *Was my brilliant plan over before it started?* she wondered. For a moment, she worried that the police might be surrounding the building. *I need more time*, she thought. She took off her shoes and tiptoed across the hall.

A dark silhouette was standing against the moonlit window.

She stepped closer and turned on the light. Her head was spinning so intensely that she saw three of him circling in her head. "Dr. Patel? What are you doing here—in my warehouse?"

"I followed you?"

"What? Look, I don't know what you want from me, but I told you that I'm not interested," Moira stated.

He strolled closer to her. There was a lab table between them. She looked up at him and got a good look at his golden brown eyes. She hadn't noticed them before. They were warm, and he smelled like Old Spice. She dropped her eyes from him and gripped the scalpel tighter.

He lifted his hands and said, "I know what you must think, but I'm not a stalker: not a threat to you. I just really want to be in your world. You're the most fascinating person I've ever seen."

"Flattery is not going to get you out of this. You had no right. And by the way, this is a little stalker-ish."

"I know. I just needed to see where you disappear off to in the evenings. I knew you weren't married or had a boyfriend, so I followed you one night. Then one night turned into two. But when you started coming here, I knew that something was up. I thought you might be in trouble until I realized what you were really doing."

"How long have you known?"

"Long enough to fall head over heels," he whispered. He came from around the table and stood inches away. "I don't know how you came up with it or why, but it is brilliant," he declared. He walked passed her and into the operating room. He was mesmerized by what Bixie stood for.

Moira sighed, dropped the scalpel into the sink, rested her hands on the edge, and pondered her next move. *I could knock him out and call the police, but then I'd have to shut down my entire operation. Or...I could let him stay and teach him what I know, just like Dr. Taylor taught me.* The former seemed to make more sense. It was all too risky. *Maybe it was for the best anyway. The neurotransmitter obviously doesn't work.*

She turned around and almost jumped out of her skin. The heart monitors and machines were in a beeping frenzy, but what was happening was far more exciting. Moira slowly stepped closer to the operating table. She slid her hand into Bixie's and gave it a soft squeeze. Bixie opened her eyes and looked up at Moira. Moira forgot to breathe. Dr. Patel was a planted fixture against the wall. His eyes almost came out of their sockets. He didn't make a sound.

It was the beginning of something wonderful.

*****

"I missed you while I was gone," Moira said.

"Same here. I'll always be grateful that you entrusted me with your most precious secret." He ran his fingers through her salt and pepper hair. Where had the time gone? Twenty years crept by yet to him she was just as beautiful as before. They had already done so much and managed to not get caught. However, he worried that their luck would eventually run out. Until then, he planned to continue their work and live every day like it was the last.

Moira reached passed him and lifted the sheet. "Who is she?"

"A new girl I found," he replied.

"We talked about this. You're not supposed to get someone new without discussing it with me first. How do I know you covered your tracks? What if someone is looking for her?"

"You said the same thing about Helidore years ago and I was right. No one came looking for her. Trust me, this girl is perfect," he explained.

"I hope you're right. I just think we should be very cautious, especially since we had the government scare a few years back. The last thing we need is to be exposed," Moira griped.

"You're right my love. That brings me to my next topic of discussion. I think we should teach the girls about our operation. I mean, obviously, they know how to kick-ass and protect us. But if they're going to be our legacy, they need to know how to perform the operations and what to look for."

"Absolutely not! They're not ready for that," Moira replied.

"Yes, they are. They're programmed to do whatever we want. We can pick one of them to be the surgeon and teach her what to do. I don't know about you, but I'm not going to live forever. I'm in my sixties and you're getting there. This is the time to prepare for the future," he said.

There it was, reality slapping her in the face—hard. Moira bit her bottom lip and sat in a nearby chair. She hated it when he was this obstinate. Even if he was right—maybe. It frustrated her that he wasn't giving her enough time to think it through. She didn't like that he already had a new prospect on the operating table without running it by her. *What else has he done that I've missed?* she wondered.

On the other hand, she had to admit that it was reckless of her not to think about the future. Then again, she had no idea if her creation would even work. Now here she was twenty years later knee-deep in something she couldn't get out of… and, even worse, she had included him in the scheme. She looked around the room and noticed the changes he'd already made. He had a hungry look in his eyes that she hadn't noticed before, probably because her own head was in the clouds.

Now her eyes were wide open and she realized that his plans were much bigger than she had ever imagined. She loved him, but now had to wonder how far would he go to get what he wanted? *Would there be a time when he couldn't be stopped?* *Absolutely,* she thought.

"Moira! What are you thinking about? Don't you hear that?" he shouted.

"Hear what?"

"That beeping sound? What is it?" he said in a panic. He checked the computer monitors and machines but couldn't figure out where the beeping was coming from.

"It's you," he hollered and grabbed her wrist. "Your watch is beeping."

Moira checked her watch and jumped out of the chair. "Oh no! It's Bixie—she flat-lined!"

Amelia

Chapter Seventeen

Amelia groaned at the blistering pain as she rested on the grass. She thought about Aaron and what he meant to her as she writhed in agony. The crippling heat was so relentless that she was certain she was being boiled alive in its intensity. She took in a few deep breaths and immediately went into a coughing fit from the smoke. She lifted her head and witnessed thick, dark plumes exuding from the water. Then it proceeded to bubble and overflow onto the grass. She moved back right before the murky water touched her skin. *Where has Bixie gone?* she wondered. Suddenly red spikes poked through the water and disappeared. She knew what that meant.

Bixie's friends would come looking soon, and they would tear her apart if they knew what she'd done. Her strategy was simple: one by one. She hid out of sight until she laid eyes on Morgan.

"Morgan," Amelia called out. She blocked Morgan's vantage point to the pond and crossed her arms. "It would save us both a lot of trouble if you could just tell me where to find Aaron. I know he's here somewhere. I can feel it."

"Where's Bixie? What did you do to her?" Morgan hissed through gritted teeth.

"I scared her off. She went looking for you," Amelia replied.

Morgan furrowed her brow and shifted her weight to one side, tapping her foot. In a split second, she lifted her hand and ran it across Amelia's face. Amelia lost her balance and toppled. With no way of breaking her fall, she landed on her shoulder. But her face felt ten times worse. She opened her mouth and closed it, hoping her jaw wasn't broken. Everything was spinning as she got back up on wobbly legs and balled her fists. She punched Morgan in the stomach and instantly cried out as the impact cracked her fingers. She glared at Morgan in shock. She had never experienced so much pain from hitting someone. *What exactly am I up against?* she pondered. She had already seen the most ungodly creatures, but never anything like this. *Who created these women?*

Morgan lifted Amelia up by her hair and threw her against a tree. *Crack!* A broken tree branch plummeted inches away from her head. She rolled over, still trying to recover. From the corner of her eye, she saw Morgan getting closer. She panicked as tears pooled her eyes. She didn't know if she would be able to figure out how to defeat a woman whose skin was indestructible. Morgan bent down and wrapped her rock hard hands around Amelia's neck. As Amelia was losing consciousness, she quickly reached for anything sharp and found a stick. It would have to do. She got a firm grip and jammed it through Morgan's eye. Morgan's hands slowly loosened and then she collapsed.

Amelia pushed her off and gasped for air.

When she was finally able to stand, she noticed that Morgan wasn't moving. She tapped her a few times with her foot for confirmation of what she already knew. Then a crimson mass poured from Morgan's face. It was over. Amelia ran as fast as she could, pushing through vines and moss, hoping to find Aaron. She screamed his name more times than she could count.

She ran until she somehow ended up back at the gate. If only she could leave. *Where could Aaron be?* she wondered. She was certain he was here. She turned around and spotted Helidore. Morgan and Bixie were piled on her shoulder like a duffel bag. She laid them side by side in the grass and pulled out her sword. Amelia prayed she wouldn't have to fight her. Helidore was too powerful. Her whole body was a solid mass of muscle. She thought about surrendering and getting the inevitable over with. Then something strange happened; that powerful feeling came back— stronger this time. It crawled through every vein and crevice inside her body, and it kept moving until she was brimming with energy.

Her vision changed so fast it scared her. Everything she laid eyes on was much clearer than before. So clear, in fact, that she could see right through inanimate objects. When she locked eyes with Helidore, she knew exactly what do and ran towards her. Power pulsed through her with such force that it was difficult to harness it, and she almost ran passed Helidore. *Concentrate*, she willed herself and slowed down. She hit Helidore head on, knocking her on her back. The sword flew into the air and landed sharp side down in the grass.

Amelia let the power take over her body and pummeled Helidore until the grass was soaked with her blood. By the time the adrenalin left Amelia's body and she came back to her senses, she noticed that Helidore was not moving. With her hands riddled with blood, she stood up and walked over to the pond. It was clear again. She looked at her reflection and jumped back. Her heart was racing as she took another look. Her eyes were glowing the brightest color blue she'd ever seen. She touched her face and wondered, *What is happening to me?*

Suddenly, another reflection appeared—Helidore.

Amelia saw everything happening in slow motion. Helidore didn't make a sound. She gripped the sword and raised it high in a perfect angle. One of her eyes was swollen shut and blood dripped from her nose into her mouth.

Amelia knew that if she didn't act quickly her life would be over. As the sword came down, she ducked and pivoted on her heels. She grabbed Helidore's waist and shoved her into the water. Helidore got a hold of Amelia's hair and pulled her in with her. She held Amelia's head underwater with great force.

Then Amelia saw him. *Am I imagining this?* she questioned. She definitely saw his face staring back at her, and it gave her strength. She kneed Helidore in the stomach and crept out of the pond.

Amelia hurried to get hold of the sword as Helidore sprang out of the water and pursued her. She turned over just as Helidore was about to lunge on top of her. The sword split Helidore's chest open.

Amelia dropped it and exhaled. She sat up and drew her knees to her chest and sobbed. It was over. Everything she had gone through was finally over. She buried her face in her hands and cried harder and harder until someone touched her hair. She looked up and jumped into Aaron's arms. She ran her fingers through his curls and stared into his beautiful green eyes. *It's really him!* she delighted.

"You're okay, love," he whispered in her ear. He put her down and took her face into his hands and kissed her. "I thought I would never see you again."

"I can't believe you're here. I feel like I moved Heaven and earth to find you," she said.

He checked her over and rubbed her arms. "I saw you walk into freezing water. I almost lost my mind. Why did you do that? Are you okay?"

"I'm okay. There was a man, he was powerful. He made me do it." Her eyes welled when Stylot came to mind. She really missed him.

"I have so much to tell you, Aaron. Some of it—you won't like," she admitted.

He shook his head and replied, "I can't believe you went through so much just to find me, and I can't wait to hear all about it. The good and the bad. But first, I have to say thank you. I don't know why this happened to us, but I know we were meant to meet and fall in love. For some reason, my life was spared, and I have a feeling yours was too. Being held here against my will gave me a lot of time to think. I now know that neither of us would've survived Leona's wrath."

Amelia held him close, rested her head on his chest, and listened to his heart beating loud and strong—just like hers.

"We're alive Aaron, and that means we can go home." She held his hands and kissed him on the lips. "And you're right. We would not have survived if certain people weren't looking out for us. From now on, our lives are what we make it. Leona will never hurt us again."

"How do you know? Is she in jail?"

Amelia shook her head no. "She's dead. Let's just say that she's getting everything she deserves."

Aaron let out a sigh of relief.

Talking about Leona reminded Amelia of leaving Joleus. She walked over to the pond and stared into the water.

"What's wrong?"

She turned to him and said, "I have to go. There's someone I need to say goodbye to."

"What? Amelia, no. You've gone through a lot to get here. We have to go."

"I can't. I can't leave without..." She sprinted to the gate and pushed it open.

Aaron followed her, picked her up, and held her over his shoulder.

"Put me down! I'm serious, I have to go back," she pleaded.

"No, I'm not letting you out of my sight again. You're gonna get yourself killed out there," he protested.

She tried to wiggle and get loose, but he repositioned her and cradled her like a baby. Amelia did everything she could to convince him to let her stay. "I'm sorry love, but we have to go."

While still holding her in his arms he kissed her forehead, closed his eyes, and jumped into the waterfall.

August 13, 2017

Moira

Chapter Eighteen

They worked until the sun set. Both Moira and Dr. Patel were mentally and physically exhausted. Never in all her medical career did Moira work as hard as she did that night. Now the two were crouched down on the operating room's floor, staring at the three women. After thirty minutes of silence, Moira burst into tears.

Dr. Patel put his arms around her and consoled her as best he could. "I'm so sorry we couldn't save them, my love. I don't understand how they could die without any warning. I mean, physically they look fine."

She lifted her head and said, "It was never supposed to be like this." She rose so quickly that she stumbled into Bixie's body. She righted herself and caressed Bixie's spiky hair. She then went over to Morgan and then Helidore. "They had no chance of survival. I thought I could save them from the evils of this world and transform them into weapons. It was amazing the way they seized the opportunity. They never asked why or demanded to leave. They loved their new life. But how could I have been so wrong? They still died," she sobbed.

He took her cold, clammy hands into his. "You gave those girls a great life Moira. What you created in that beautiful brain of yours is magnificent. They never had much of a life before they met you. Neither of us can explain why they died, but we can be assured that the last twenty years of their lives were happy ones."

She loved that he always knew exactly what to say. But the pain and emptiness she felt were much greater than he could console, and it was eating away at her. *How can I live with myself knowing that three young girls lost their lives while in my care?* she lamented. *Maybe they were better off dying years ago by natural causes instead of by my interferences.* She ran to the sink and heaved.

He went over to her and pulled her hair from her face. He comforted her as she vomited her emotions away.

"I'm a terrible person," she moaned, panting for air.

"No, you're not. You loved those girls, and your heart was in the right place," he insisted.

"That may be true, but it doesn't change what happened here tonight."

He patted her on the shoulder and then went over and covered each girl's body with a sheet.

Moira left the operating room and sat on the large couch in the lounge. She wanted to disappear off the face of the earth. No matter what he said, she knew that there was no way she would get over what had happened. Her eyes welled with tears again. Tired and heartbroken, she curled up and stared out the window until her mind drifted away.

*****

The next morning, she woke up to the smell of fresh coffee brewing across the room. After fixing herself a cup, she reluctantly went inside the operating room and stopped in her tracks. The cup fell from her grasp and shattered. The spilled coffee burned her legs as it splashed on the floor. She couldn't move or speak. The girls were gone. Everything was spotless and sterile as if nothing had ever happened. For a second she thought last night was a dream. But the pain in her heart told her a different story. She looked all over for him and stopped in front of the side door that led to the basement. She didn't want to go down there, especially since her girls were no longer there, but it was the only place she hadn't checked. She slowly took the winding stairs down and paused when she heard whispering.

When she took the last step, she couldn't believe her eyes: a girl was lying on a table. She was unconscious and hooked up to a machine. Dr. Patel was talking into a recorder about his research. Her worst fears were coming true.

"What's going on here?" she asked.

He looked at her, and his mouth flew open. "Hey, I wanted to surprise you. This is Cheryl."

Moira rolled her eyes and turned to leave.

"Wait! Don't go," he pleaded.

"You have gone way too far this time. I'm shutting this all down. It's over! Return this girl to wherever you found her before someone gets wind of us and what we're doing," she demanded.

He crossed his arms and pursed his lips. "No. We're not shutting this down. We still have a lot to do and more lives to save. Look, I know where this is coming from. You're angry that I got rid of the girls, aren't you?"

"This has nothing to do with the girls. It's about learning from our mistakes and doing the right thing. I had no business doing what I did, and I will spend the rest of my life regretting it." She wiped a rolling tear and whispered, "I hate that you were brought into this."

"I wasn't brought into it. I found you here, remember? When I followed you that night and saw what you were doing, it was like stumbling upon a gold mine. I needed to be a part of it. Trust me, Cheryl is a new beginning for us. She can continue our legacy if the implant works," he explained.

"That's a big if. The last girl you hijacked didn't make it through the surgery. No. This has to stop. Now! We can't risk any more lives. I'm putting an end to this calamity—with or without your help." She marched up the stairs, stopped at the top one, turned and said, "And by the way, what did you do with the girls?"

"I put them in our freezer until we could give them a proper burial," he muttered.

*****

Moira pledged that no matter what might happen in the future, she was done playing God with people's lives. She wanted to be able to look at herself in the mirror again without being repulsed. *Dr. Taylor would be so disappointed in me*, she thought. *He would've expected me to do things the right way, the way he taught me.*

That night, she kissed Dr. Patel goodnight and slipped out of bed.

He would never approve of what she was about to do, but it needed to be done. For so many reasons, she had to find peace, and she knew that this was the only way.

"Dr. Smith, I must say that's a heck of a story. Are you feeling okay?" Officer Richards asked. He looked into her bloodshot eyes and asked, "Have you been drinking?"

"I can show you," she responded with confidence.

He took her in his patrol car, and before too long there was a team of forensic technicians, detectives, and EMTs surrounding Moira's warehouse. She sat quietly in the passenger side of Officer Richard's patrol car and stared out into the night sky. The stars were so bright and soothing. She let her imagination run wild and tried to ignore the relevance of her current reality. The impending catastrophe, losing her husband, and her freedom weighed heavily on her, but she still

155

didn't regret any of it. She sat back and rested her hands behind her head with a big smile on her face.

"Moira, wake up!" a voice shouted.

She yawned and stepped out of the patrol car. She was more tired than she thought. She turned around and put her hands behind her back.

"What are you doing?" Officer Richards asked.

She frowned and looked over her shoulder. "Well? Aren't you going to arrest me?"

"I suggest you go get some sleep, Dr. Smith. There is nothing inside your warehouse that causes any suspicion. You are free to go."

"Free to go? No, there are bodies in there! Did you check the freezer?"

"Your husband said you worked twelve hours straight and that you haven't been getting much sleep," he replied.

"Listen to me, I know what I'm talking about," she insisted. As the words fluttered out of her mouth, she noticed patrol cars and detectives driving away. Officer Richards patted her on the shoulder and got in his car.

Furious, she marched into the warehouse and found Dr. Patel in the lab. He was humming along to Samuel Barber without a care in the world. She slammed the door shut and turned off the music.

"What the hell have you done?" she yelled.

He narrowed his eyes and leaned over the desk. "What do you mean?"

She stepped closer and slammed her hands on the desk. "Don't you dare play innocent with me. I was ready to turn myself in, and you go and get rid of all the evidence. How did you even know what I was going to do?"

"I knew the moment we lost the girls. You had this look in your eye, and I needed to come up with a backup plan...for both of us," he explained.

"It wasn't up to you. You wouldn't listen to me, and I had to stop you before it was too late."

"I'll admit I didn't want to stop, but I did what you asked. I returned Cheryl to the hospital without anyone noticing. Then I removed any evidence that would incriminate us, and I put the girls in a safe place."

Moira ran her fingers through her hair and sat down. Her head was spinning. She bit her bottom lip and thought hard about what to do next.

He walked over and kneeled in front of her. He lifted her chin. "I did it because I can't live without you, and I was not going to stand by and watch you go to prison when I knew that your heart was in the right place. You wanted to give those girls a chance...you cared."

"I just—I don't know what to do. How can I go on like nothing ever happened?" she asked.

"We don't go on like nothing ever happened. But we can make it right. No more underground work. From now on, we do our research in the hospitals, and we put in the hours to perfect the neurotransmitters. No more illegal experimentation," he said.

She stared into his eyes and knew he was being honest. "Really? I never thought you would be willing to go legit. I mean, you were so obstinate before."

"Nothing is more important to me than you. I would follow you to the ends of the earth," he whispered and then planted a long kiss on her lips.

That night, they put Bixie, Morgan, and Helidore in their final resting place.

Amelia

Chapter Nineteen

The sweet aroma of peonies and roses was the first thing Amelia noticed as her mind slowly stepped into reality. It was a long time coming. If only her body would follow suit. She couldn't move her arms or legs, and there was so much pain radiating from her chest. People were whispering and doing a terrible job at being discreet. She even heard the news reporter blaring about the local weather on the television. Then she felt someone slip warm hands into hers. It sent electric waves throughout her body, as if each part of her insides were being switched on.

"Amelia, honey, it's time for you to wake up."

Someone kissed her cheek. "That's right sleeping beauty. We need you to stay here with us."

The two very distinct voices were all she needed to hear. Every part of her was connected to them, and her body was not going to fail her now. Her eyes slowly cracked open. Two blurry faces were staring back at her. She blinked a few times, and the faces appeared.

"M-mom, Dad?" she croaked.

Alexandria's face lit up as she held tight to Amelia's hand. Cash bent down and wrapped his arms around her. "I'm going to go get the doctor," Alexandria said.

Cash sat back down and wiped a running tear. "They say men aren't supposed to cry," he said through a laugh. He reached for her hand and scooted closer. "Thank you for saving my life. I don't know if I'd be alive if it weren't for you. No one would ever believe our story," he whispered.

She nodded and attempted to speak, but her throat was as dry as sandpaper. Alexandria came back with a team of nurses and Dr. Wallis. He shined a light in her eyes and listened to her lungs through his stethoscope. She mustered the strength to follow all of his commands by moving different parts of her body. He removed his eyeglasses and rubbed the bridge of his nose.

"Amelia, you are a very lucky girl. Your vitals look good, and there is no permanent damage. The bullet just missed your lungs by a few inches," Dr. Wallis stated. He patted her on the shoulder. "We're glad to have you back."

"Thank you, doctor, for everything," Alexandria said.

One by one, four nurses gave Amelia a hug and wished her well. She was confused but went along with it. After taking a small sip of water and clearing her throat, she whispered, "Aaron?"

"He's fine honey, more than fine. He was discharged two weeks ago. He's been here every day wishing you well," Alexandria murmured. She noticed Cash was still talking to Dr. Wallis and whispered, "He's a cutie-pie, by the way."

Amelia laughed and then went into a coughing fit. Alexandria patted her back and poured her more water.

"Is she alright?" Cash asked, rushing over.

"She's okay. Just needs to take it easy." She winked at Amelia.

"Where's Navid?" Amelia asked.

Just as she said the words, he appeared in the doorway. He ran over and wrapped his arms around her. She squeezed him as hard as she could as they both sobbed. He finally pulled back and wiped his nose. "Don't ever do that to me again. I have to see a psychiatrist now because of you."

Amelia giggled and shrugged her shoulders as rivulets crept down her cheeks.

"You kept your promise. I will never forget it," she said.

"How was your sleep?"

"Disastrous at best, but there were a lot of good parts," she replied and winked at Cash. He smiled back and put his arm around Alexandria.

"I'll bet. Hey, there was something I wanted to ask you. Months ago, we got you to wake up for a minute, and you mentioned my father. Did you see him? Was he…"

She took his hand and said, "Roland wanted you to know how much he loves you, and he's very proud."

His bottom lip quivered. "Thank you. I think I really needed to hear that." He sniffed and rubbed his tired eyes. He gave her one more hug and left.

After a long nap, Amelia awoke with a start. Cash and Alexandria were sound asleep right next to her bed. *It's real. It's not a dream*, she told herself. She had given up hope a long time ago, but as luck would have it, she was back with her family again. And this time there would be no Leona lurking to mess things up. Aaron was okay, and all was right in the world.

While deep in her thoughts about her future, she heard the breaking news announcement on the television and turned up the volume. It was intriguing to learn how much she missed while unconscious, and realized at that moment that there was nothing more normal than watching the news. She embraced normal after the crazy ride she just had.

"I'm Janine Morales here at Riverleaf Hospital with some exciting news. Dr. Moira Smith and Dr. Kavi Patel have created a ground-breaking medical phenomenon." The camera closed in on a tiny device that resembled a plastic hearing aid. "What you're looking at folks is a neurotransmitter. This little miracle is the future of medicine. It can basically signal all parts of the body and act as a brain, which is important for those who experience brain trauma or head injuries." The reporter pointed the microphone at Moira and said, "What would you like the world to know about your brilliant creation Dr. Smith."

As Dr. Smith spoke, Amelia was practically on the edge of the bed. Her heart was racing, and her palms and armpits started to sweat. There was something in Dr. Smith's eyes that wasn't right. It was guilt. After what Amelia had just been through, she could spot it a mile away. She never thought she would find the moron who created those girls…and there she was, live on television.

"I'll be watching you—Moira," Amelia whispered.

*****

Three days later, Amelia was finally set to go home. Alexandria helped her out of bed, and a yellow rock fell out of the sheets. It sparkled like a firework.

"Wow, what is this?" Alexandria said while peering at the flickering edges. "I've never seen anything like it."

"That's because it's not from here," Amelia said as her lips quivered. She burst into tears. To her, the stone represented a promise he'd made to her. *One that he should've made to someone else more deserving,* she thought. *I'll never forgive myself for leaving with no explanation.*

Alexandria held Amelia in her arms until the sobs turned into sniffles. When her daughter had composed herself, she dressed, collected her things, and they left the hospital.

When they finally pulled up to the house, Amelia couldn't believe how beautiful it still looked on the outside. She assumed in some weird way that it would've melted or imploded. When Cash opened the door, Amelia could smell the sweet aroma of fresh baked brownies and comfort food.

"Surprise!"

She jumped back and almost fell from the excitement. A big *Welcome Home* banner was splayed across the living room ceiling along with colorful balloons and streamers. But most of all, there were a lot of smiling faces. She was relieved to see one in particular.

She ran into Aaron's arms. They stood and held each other for as long as they could.

She finally looked up at him and stared into his green eyes. For so long those eyes had been her home, a guiding light, and seeing them now meant that everything was going to be okay. He kissed her on the lips and walked her out to their favorite tree. A blanket and food were waiting for them. She grinned and carefully sat down. Her body did not let her forget she had just been through tremendous trauma. But the welcoming breeze was just as perfect as it always had been. It calmed her.

They toasted to life and held each other close.

That night, after everyone left and went home, Amelia was alone in her room when she heard a knock on her back door. To her surprise, it was Aaron.

"Hey, I thought you had gone," Amelia said.

He strolled in and kissed her on the cheek. "I wanted to talk to you about something important."

She sat down and patted the empty space next to her. "What's on your mind?"

He took her hand and said, "Lisette, I want you to come with me."

"Come with you? Where are you going?"

He stood up and cracked his knuckles. Then he paced back and forth until she got up and stood directly in front of him.

He sighed and put his hands on both her arms, almost as if he needed support to stand. "I'm leaving," he finally muttered.

Amelia stepped back, her heart raced.

"I talked to my father about this weeks ago. After what happened with mom—he gave me his blessing. What I want is to live my life to the fullest. I'm gonna travel the world and see what's out there and explore new things."

She looked up at him. "I'm so happy for you Aaron," she said with tears in her eyes. "Really, I am. That's what Gisel would've wanted. We both got a second chance at life, and I don't think we should waste a moment of it."

He knelt down in front of her and took her hands. "Then you'll come with me?"

The tears rippled down her face. She shook her head no. It killed her to see the heartbreak in his eyes. "I just got my life back, Aaron. I want to finish school, and maybe go to college. I want to spend more time with my parents," she explained.

"I suppose I don't blame you. You were stolen from your life, and it wouldn't be fair of me to pressure you into leaving."

"Thank you for understanding," she whispered.

"Mom came to me you know." Amelia's eyes brightened at the thought of Gisel and the sacrifice she made for her son. "She told me to live every day like there was no tomorrow, and that she loved me very much," he said.

"I'm so glad she did. I want you to know that you will always be an important part of my life."

He lifted her in his arms and kissed her passionately. "You went through hell and back just to save my life. Lisette, I will love you for the rest of my life. No matter where you are or what you're doing—don't ever forget that."

"I love you too. And I'm going to miss you so much," Amelia replied. She ran her fingers through his curls one last time.

He cupped her chin and kissed her lips once more before they tearfully said goodbye.

He opened the door and turned to look at her one last time. She stared into his indelible green eyes and blew him a kiss.

Amelia

Chapter Twenty

"Good morning, sweetheart. Rise and shine." Alexandria sauntered in Amelia's room and went straight for the window.

Amelia smirked and covered her head with her blanket.

Alexandria opened the curtains and drew the blinds.

Cash entered behind and sat on the edge of the bed. He pulled back the blanket and waved. She forgot how corny her parents could be.

"Dad, you look well rested," she said

"Ha! You have no idea," he replied.

"I know, it's the strangest thing. He hasn't had a single nightmare. In fact, I woke up a few times to make sure he was still alive," Alexandria quipped. Cash shot Amelia a quick glance, and they both laughed. "What's so funny?"

"Let's just say the monster in Dad's nightmares is gone for good," Amelia declared. "Speaking of dreams, there is something I need to tell you guys." She sat up and crossed her arms. She pondered the best delivery on such a depressing topic and was a little annoyed that they never confided in her about it.

"What is it, honey?" Alexandria probed.

"I don't know if you guys are aware, but I flat-lined in the hospital. Within that time I went to Heaven, and I think I met my brother."

Alexandria and Cash's eyes were suddenly ages away. They were catapulted to that horrible day from their past. Alexandria recollected every detail, even the pain. Her heart broke all over again. Cash ran his fingers through his hair and pursed his lips. The anger he managed to bury years ago was mounting to the surface.

Alexandria touched his hand and cried, "We had a boy, and he's in Heaven." She struggled to remain calm.

"Yes, and he's beautiful. He looks just like me," Amelia said. "I hope it's okay that I named him. His name is Andrew."

Alexandria reached out her arms. Amelia climbed into them. "It's perfect," she whispered, twirling a strand of her daughter's hair.

"Now on a more serious note…what's for breakfast?" Amelia said, wiping her eyes.

"Let's go out. We've never been to Columbia, Missouri before. Maybe afterward we can do some shopping before we pack up and head to Stillwater," Alexandria replied.

"In a strange way, I feel like this is my home now. I love this house, and I don't think I want to go back to Stillwater."

"What about your friends? Won't you miss being in your own element again?" Cash asked.

"I can always go back and visit them. I'd like to finish high school early if I can and maybe go to college here."

"I don't know honey, there are so many terrible memories in this place. I mean, Leona kidnapped you and tortured you and Aaron. Won't being here be a reminder of a horrible time in your life?" Alexandria inquired.

Her mom made some valid points, but there was no place she'd rather be.

"What I'll remember is that I fell in love with a guy named Aaron who saved me, and in turn I saved him. I'll remember that Navid is more of a brother to me now, and his fiancée is a sister. I'll remember that Leona will never hurt any of us again. This is where I want to start my new life."

Cash and Alexandria placated her and gave her some time before they made any final decisions. Before too long, when they realized their daughter wouldn't budge, Cash relocated his construction business and Alexandria started a new job teaching at the local college.

*****

On Amelia's eighteenth birthday, she received a postcard from Aaron. He was in Scotland. He took a picture of himself in front of a castle. His face was lit up like a starry sky. She could feel his happiness bouncing off the photos, and it made her laugh. She had her family and her life back, but she never looked like Aaron did in the picture. She was missing something in her life, and she knew what it was, but it was impossible.

For a year she dreamed of searching for Joleus. Every night she got closer and closer to the wooden door, but she could never get inside. And every morning she awoke disappointed that she couldn't get to him. It was devastating. She assumed that they banned her from the existence for all eternity. But she still went to bed every night thinking about him and the Sigans. The most magical place in her dreams would soon be nothing more than a memory, and that reality tortured her every day.

One night, she put the rock under her pillow and dreamed of walking to the door. She put her hand on the knob, expecting it to disappear like all of the other times before, but this time it opened. She stood there, wondering if someone was waiting to kill her on the other end. Whatever lurked on the other side didn't frighten her enough to leave. She stepped inside of Sigmount. The door shut behind her. She had tears in her eyes and the rock in her hand. She was finally getting the chance to apologize for leaving. The large fruit tree was beckoning her to come closer. She picked a green apple and savored it down to the core. The sweet juice was addictive as it ran down her lips. She thought about getting another one when someone tapped her on the shoulder. She turned around and knelt down to hug a Sigan. She was delighted that they remembered her.

They wouldn't speak but pointed in the direction of Zerios. She took a deep breath and entered the forest. The walk was comforting and nostalgic. She remembered the smell of the trees and the mouthwatering aroma of the flowers. She laughed while thinking about the bouquet of roses he gave her, and the baths they took in the pond. She was so lost in thought she didn't realize she was already there.

"Amelia!" Briseus squealed as she galloped over. Amelia wrapped her arms around her neck and kissed her cheek. "I missed you," she said.

"I missed you too. You've gotten so big," Amelia replied. From afar she saw the King and Chara engaged in conversation with a few Zerians. Eric was ecstatic and jumping up and down after speaking with the king. Amelia couldn't help but wonder why he was so happy. There was even a smile on his face. He had always been serious that it caused her to question if he even had teeth.

"I have to go. I'm having dinner with my friends," Briseus whispered. She rested her head on Amelia's shoulder and walked away.

"Hey, before you go, where is Joleus?" Amelia called after her.

"He's not here," she answered back and disappeared into the forest.

Not here? Crap, now what? she said to herself. Then she figured that maybe he had gone home for the day. She paused when she realized he may be with someone—after all, Chara had been in a hurry to get him married. Nonetheless, she ran to his home and searched the perimeter. He wasn't there either. Saddened, she walked around and stumbled upon the message she left him in the dirt. It was still there. Her eyes stung and flooded with tears. She sobbed so hard it woke her up. Her words haunted him every day? It made her cry harder, knowing that he suffered by seeing that ridiculous message day in and day out. And now there was no going back. It was four o'clock in the morning when she finally calmed herself down.

Later that afternoon, she was watching television with her parents when the doorbell rang. She opened the door to a large bouquet of pink roses.

"Oh no! Cash, I swear I'm not having an affair," Alexandria joked.

Cash squeezed her in his arms and kissed her lips. "I know dear, I know," he said.

Amelia took the roses and waited for the gentleman to get his clipboard and turn around.

The wind blew at the perfect pace, and the sun gleamed off the strands in his hair. Her heart pounded against her chest. He turned around and looked down as he handed Amelia a box. She took it and waited for him to look up.

Alexandria and Cash came up behind her. "Who are they from?" Alexandria asked.

Amelia froze. She couldn't speak or move until the man looked at her. He finally lifted his face and stared into her eyes.

"Joleus?" Amelia whispered. She said it so low only the two of them could hear.

His lips parted enough to utter, "I asked you a question that deemed a response. I said I would get my answer."

Amelia jumped into his arms and they both fell in the grass. She kissed every inch of his face. He laughed and held her close as they got back up. He picked up the box and got down on one knee. Tears ran down her face. She was shaking.

"Amelia Lisette Waters, will you marry me?"

"Yes! I will marry you," she cried as he slid a bright yellow diamond on her finger.

"Who the hell is that?" Cash whispered.

"I don't know. I thought you knew," Alexandria replied. They closed the door and waited inside.

"How is this possible? I searched every night for you for a year," she cried. "I'm so sorry I left you. And then I saw the message I left you still in the dirt…"

He put his finger on her lips and shook his head. "It's okay Amelia. That message was all I had left of you, that's why I kept it. I knew you had to save Aaron. I just wished you would've let me go with you. I wanted to protect you," he explained.

"I know, but I couldn't take that risk. Thank goodness Aaron and I made it out in one piece."

He dug his shoe in the dirt and twisted his lips. "So how is our friend Aaron? Is he somewhere far away?"

Amelia giggled and rolled her eyes. "Yes, he's happy and somewhere far away."

She rubbed her temples and wiped the tears from her face. "I still can't believe you're here. How is this possible?" She pointed down and said, "You have legs."

Joleus nodded and replied, "Yeah, I don't think I would've made it far had I showed up half-horse. My parents granted my wish and gave us their blessing. A little magic I suppose. We're lucky."

"Indeed," she whispered, wrapping her arms around his neck. They kissed for so long their bodies practically melted.

"We should probably table this for now," he quipped as their lips still touched.

"We were going to spend that special night together, before the raid," Amelia recalled. "Do you think we can still experience your way?"

Joleus blushed. "I'm sure we still can. I may have a little magic left. But I would like to experience the human way first. It's so personal and intimate. I read all about it before I came here."

"Glad to see you did your homework. Hey, will you see your parents again? I mean, can they come here or…"

"We can see them in our dreams. That was one of the stipulations, that no matter what, I have to visit often…in my dreams."

He pulled her into his arms and swung her around. "I have one more surprise," he said.

"As if you being here isn't surprising enough. I love you so much, Joleus."

"Hold that thought." He ran to his car and pulled out a little black puppy, barking joyfully.

Amelia fell to her knees as it ran and jumped into her arms. She looked at Joleus in shock. "Stylot?" It stopped barking and licked her face. "Oh my…how?"

I followed you as far as I could go and found him. But the only way we could bring him back was as a puppy.

She hugged his little furry neck and kissed the top of his head. "I have never been happier than I am right now," she confessed, rubbing Stylot's belly.

Joleus wiped a tear from her face. "That's all I want for you, my sweet. And I love you, too."

They walked hand in hand into the house with Stylot trailing behind.

"Mom, Dad, this is Joleus," Amelia said.

Epilogue

They were standing under a crystal blue sky. The sun let off just enough heat to make the day unforgettable—not that Amelia ever would. Music set the mood. Although Joleus was human now, he still looked too perfect. His luxurious hair had grown a few more inches and she'd swear his blue eyes were brighter than before. She found herself staring often to the point of embarrassment. Thankfully for her, he hardly ever noticed. The freshly picked bouquet of wildflowers calmed her nerves as she strolled down the aisle. Each step she took felt like she was walking on a cloud, and her gown brushed the ground as she stepped closer and closer to the front.

They were directly across from each other, and it felt like they were the only two people in the world. She couldn't wait to spend the rest of her life with him. She found herself smiling for no reason and even winked at him a few times as they stood in silence. He whispered something to her, but she couldn't make it out. She furrowed her brow and mouthed the words *what's wrong?*

Joleus pointed down, but she couldn't figure out what he was saying.

"Amelia? The rings?" Navid whispered.

"Oh, sorry," she said, handing them over. Some giggles escaped the crowd as her face flushed. For the rest of the ceremony, she opted to not look at Joleus.

Later that evening, Amelia and Joleus walked onto the dance floor and held each other close.

"You look very beautiful tonight," he said, twirling her around.

"And you look very handsome. Sometimes I can't stop staring. You look like you don't belong here."

He chuckled and put his hand on the small of her back. "Where do I belong then, my sweet?"

"With me," she sighed, kissing him.

"May I cut in?" Navid asked.

"Of course. Just give her back," Joleus joked.

"I like him; he's good for you. You guys match," Navid said.

"I know, it's so strange the way we connected. It's like we didn't need time to realize our feelings because they were already there."

"That's how it should be. I knew the moment I met Sharon that she was the one. And now we're finally married."

"I'm so happy for you, Navid. I want nothing but the best for you," Amelia said. "Oh, and I'm sorry for being the worst best man…girl."

"You were perfect. It's cute the way you and Joleus are together. How did you meet again?"

"It's a long story," Amelia replied. "Maybe one day I'll tell you about my adventures."

"I look forward to it." A sudden gloom came over him and he tensed up. They stopped dancing.

"What's wrong?" Amelia asked.

"I wanted to be the first to let you know. I heard from Brady, he said Eli was sentenced to life in prison without parole," he confessed.

"Oh. I don't know what to say. I'm sorry if you're hurting."

"He brought it on himself, Amelia. I stood up to Mom and he could've done the same thing, but he didn't. I just— wanted more from him, you know. A part of me will always blame myself for not trying hard enough to break that demented connection they had."

"I understand, but let's not forget that I was there, too. He was his mother's son. There was nothing any of us could've done. Plus, you were dealing with demons of your own. Your childhood was stolen because of her," she said.

"That's true. I'm just glad it brought us closer. Now we can both be free and happy. That brings me to a question I have to ask?"

"Oh boy, what is it?"

"How would Joleus and you like to go with Sharon and me on our honeymoon?"

"That sounds weird. Don't you guys want to be alone?"

"Sharon's parents rented out this huge villa for us in Hawaii. Trust me, it will be fun. You can even bring that mutt if you want," he joked.

"Excuse you, his name is Stylot."

Navid laughed and put his hands in praying form. "Come on, we all need this after the year we've had. It was Sharon's idea by the way, so you have to say yes. You can't tell the bride no on her wedding day."

Joleus snuck up behind Amelia and placed his hands on her waist.

She turned to him and asked, "Wanna go to Hawaii?"

"Are you kidding? When do we leave?" he said as he planted a kiss. She gave Navid a thumbs up before he whisked his bride in his arms. "When we get back we can start planning our own wedding," Joleus declared.

"I can't wait," she replied as they danced the night away.

After a long jilted road and many mountains climbed, Amelia finally got her happily ever after with the man from her dreams. Her life was complete, and she intended to live out the rest of her days in Joleus's arms.

The End

Acknowledgments

The Like a Dream Series is one of the proudest works I've done and I'm so excited that it is complete and ready to be devoured by my readers. I thank God every day for the gift I've been given, and my love for writing grows more and more each day.

I want to thank my husband Hilton, who has always been supportive and loving. My kids Laila and Josiah are my solace and my motivation.

Thank you to my mother, for your love and prayers, and for always believing in me.

A special thanks to my friends and family who have been a constant in my life and for reading every crazy word I've written.

To my editor, Mindy Reed, thank you for taking a chance on a new writer like myself, and for making *Waking Amelia* better than before. Your talent is truly is amazing.

To my publicist Danielle, I appreciate everything you do for me. You've been a lifesaver when it comes to promotions, advice, and just helping me come into my own as an author. I'm happy to call you a friend.

Thanks to designer James Egan, for the incredible book covers. You took a thought and turned it into something better than I could've imagined.

$\mathcal{S}$HINA JAMES is the author of the Like a Dream

Series. She resides in the state of Texas with her husband and two kids. When she's not writing or reading life-changing novels, she loves traveling, listening to music, and cooking.

Visit SHINA JAMES at:

www.shinajames.com

facebook.com/authorshinajames

TWITTER- @shina_j1

Jacket Design by:

James Egan with Bookfly Design